Saved: Annabelle's Beginning

C. Caldwell

Acknowledgments

I would like to take a moment to give a special thanks to those who have helped me through this process. To my mentor Cederick Stewart, thank you for the late-night reviews, editing, and allowing me to ask too many questions. To my mother, thank you for being an inspiring role model and motivating me to continue this journey. Thank you for pushing me to be the best person I can be. I can now say and believe that when you put your mind to something, you can accomplish anything.

Chapter 1

My bare feet crunched under the leaves as I ran for my life. I was afraid, but I didn't know why. The moon shined bright in the baby blue sky, as it awaits the arrival of the sun. I was running in what appeared to be a forest. The trees were bare, brittle, and shadowed. It was like something you'd see in a black and white horror film.

"You shouldn't have come here..." I hear a someone yell out in the distance. The tone was harsh and it held authority. It made me flinch because it reminded me of my dad. I glance behind me hoping to find the owner of the voice but was unsuccessful when I spot nothing but trees and dead leaves.

"Yeah, well she's here now, so you'll just have to deal with it." I heard a familiar boyish voice say that sounded like it was coming from my left. I look in the direction it came from but was unsuccessful again in locating its' owner. What's going on?

"This is going to cause unwanted attention to this family! I'm pulling the plug!" I hear that same voice shout with authority. Pull the plug?

"No!" I hear the same familiar boyish voice yell, followed by commotion. It sounded like they were fighting. The sound of glass breaking was all that I could hear. I gasp as I come in close contact with a hanging branch from a tree. I quickly dodge the branch and come to a stop as I approach a cliff. I look down to see the black water, as the waves rose and fell, crashing into the side of the cliff. I'm interrupted when I hear what sounds like people running, followed by several animalistic growls. I turn around to see a black figure emerge from behind a tree a few feet in front of me. This shadow appeared to be a man. I see a flash of light being reflected off something in his hand. I squint in attempt to see what he was holding. Once my eyes adjusted, I noticed that "something", was a gun. My heart began to race and I couldn't catch my breath. Out of the corners of my eyes, I could see more shadows emerging from the trees.

"You shouldn't have come here..." They all say in unison.

"No, please!" I begged. The man slowly raises his arm, pointing the gun in my direction. "No, don't shoot." I whispered in a voice that was unfamiliar to me. I hear the gun cock back.

I'm awakened from slumber by my head bumping into the glass window of my dad's truck as he goes over a bump in the road. Thank god that was just a dream. My heart still raced in my chest as if it were real. I could feel sweat rolling down my back. I nearly jump as I hear my dad chuckle at me. I had fallen asleep on the way home from my high-school orientation. It was an hour and forty-five minutes away from the actual school. This was something every student had to attend before the first day of school.

"That outta teach you not to fall asleep in my truck." My dad says in his normal harsh tone. I look over at him just as he puts on his signal light. His facial expression was harsh as usual. Not a glimpse of happiness. Once we were on Maple street, he begins to remind me of the do's and don'ts for my junior year. My favorite is: "Just because you're a junior doesn't mean you can start talking to girls...or boys for that matter. No boys... You go to school to learn. Nothing less than that." Instead of replying to him, I turn my head and watch as the rain droplets fall onto the window. Really? What boy would want to talk to me? We pass a couple of kids running around jumping with glee. They had something I clearly would never have. Happiness. It was taken from me in the fifth grade and I remember that day like it was yesterday. March 12th is when it happened. My dad came to surprise me after school on my birthday. He took me out for ice cream at that old Dairy Queen, the one he and my mom went to when they were dating. When we arrived home, my mom wasn't there. I figured she was hiding and trying to pick the right moment to jump out and scare me like she usually did. Apparently, that wasn't the case because the look on my dad's face told me otherwise. In his hand, he held a pink piece of paper. Tears ran down his face like a waterfall, as he stared at whatever was on that paper. I start to get a lump in my throat, feeling the sudden up rise of panic. It takes me a few seconds to gather up the courage to ask him what was on my mind. He slowly puts the note down on the small round table next to the staircase. His facial expression was a mix of shock and pain.

"What's wrong dad?" I ask while stepping forward. His head snapped up and just like that, the shock and pained expression on his face was replaced with anger. His face began to turn a bright red. I look into his green piercing eyes only to see the anger swirling within them. He points his finger at me and shouts.

"You! You're what's wrong! You're the reason she left!" I flinch being startled by his outburst. He had never yelled at me like that before and to be honest, it hurt.

"M-me? W-why would she leave b-b-because of me?" I stuttered in fear.

"Money and struggling to take care of you! Do you know how long we struggled to keep this family together? Huh? The food on that table we've worked our butts off for? You see, I knew... I *knew* we should've given you up, but your mother wouldn't let you out of her grip." He snarled at me. I could see veins popping out of his neck. Why would they want to get rid of me? Their *own* flesh and blood? Am I not good enough for them? Was I that much of a disappointment, that my own mother walked out on us? On *me*? My vision got blurry and for a moment I didn't know what was happening until I felt something warm rolling down my cheeks. I felt anger boil up inside me as he continued to shout at me. This feeling was foreign to me because I always had something to smile about. I gave into this new feeling and before I could stop myself, I said three words I never imagined myself saying.

"I hate you!" I screamed at the top of my lungs and the moment those words slipped passed my lips, I knew I was in big trouble. I didn't have much time to fully register what came out of my mouth, because I was being dragged across the hallway and into the kitchen. I tried to fight him off but he was too strong for me. Before I knew it, peanut butter was being shoved down my throat. He kicked me in the stomach forcing me to swallow the sweet and dry textured peanut butter. He knew I was allergic but that didn't stop him. He left me there as I gasped for air. The sharp pain in my stomach kept me on the floor. In a matter of seconds, everything slowly became dim. I continued to cling to the little energy I had, trying so desperately to get air into my lungs. Out of the corner of my eye, I see my dad's blurry figure moving through the kitchen drawers searching for something. He approached me and I felt a pinch on my thigh. My epi-pen! Maybe he wasn't going to leave me to die after all. Within seconds, I feel my throat slowly unclench itself, allowing me to breathe. My dad grabbed me roughly by my hair which brought me to stand up groaning.

"You will never say those words to me *ever* again, and if you ever tell anyone what happened, I, *will,* kill you." he threatened me. He then roughly releases me, making sure to give me a little shove. He stormed off leaving me alone in the kitchen. I fall on the floor as I choked out a sob. Ever since that day, I haven't uttered a single word. I haven't smiled or laughed. Come to think of it, I don't think I even know what my voice sounds like anymore. I'm brought back from the memories of that dreadful day once I hear my dad's loud voice.

"Annabelle! Get out, you're wasting the amount of time it's going to take before I can get my meal." My dad says clearly growing impatient. I almost flinch as I see we are parked outside our blue and white Victorian style home. This wouldn't be the first time I've been so caught up in my thoughts, that I'm oblivious to my surroundings. I get out of the truck and start approaching the door. The squeaking metal on the porch swing reminds of the many times I sat there laughing with my mom. I open the door and the stench of beer is everywhere. That explains why my dad's in a sour mood. I drop my red folder off on the small round table in the hallway, that's on the side of the staircase. I make my way pass the living room and into the kitchen. I'm greeted by an overly large yet long brown rectangle-shaped kitchen table, big enough to seat 6 with only two chairs. One nice sturdy plush chair and one beat up mismatched chair that doesn't belong in the mist of anyone's company (I'm pretty sure we could guess who sits in what chair). Across from the table was the white door that led to the back-yard. I've ran through that door dressed in dirt so many times to see the look of shock on my mom's face as I left dirt prints on her clean tile floors. She would only burst out laughing when she saw the condition I was in. I can still remember the times when I'd bring in frogs from the yard and my mom would threaten to fix them for dinner saying, "Well dear, it really does taste like chicken". I smile at that. I can even recall when my mom had dad place that black cloth to cover the small diamond shaped window that was on the back door because of my fear of lighting. I head towards the black refrigerator to prep dad's dinner. There were so many great memories in this kitchen, but that changed once mom left. Now, all there ever is, are bad memories. Next to refrigerator was the countertop where the cabinet door still had a crack in the wood from when my dad through me into it because I was too slow at fixing his dinner. Which reminds me that I need it speed up. I'm so thankful for the black gas stove because it is my saving grace as it cuts down my cooking time. I sit the chicken on the white counter top between the stove and the sink and open the pantry door. I search for the pasta and when I find it, I smile. My feet hurt from standing so long in the orientation lines today, that I ache to feel the cool comfort of the white diamond shape tiled kitchen floor. Our kitchen wasn't great, but it was better than nothing. I wash my hands and make my way to the pantry to grab the remaining ingredients. Twenty minutes later, dinner is served: sautéed chicken, fettuccini, garlic bread, and a tossed salad. I fix my dad's plate and set it on the table just as he walks in.

"Hm. It almost smells good down here...almost..." he trails off as he takes a seat in his chair.

"Jerk" I mentally think as I began cleaning the kitchen. I'm not allowed to eat until he's finished with his meal. What kind of parent does that to their own child, their *only* child? Then again, he's been everything but a parent to me. He likes to pretend that mom leaving us only affects him. He doesn't even know the half of it. He doesn't understand me like mom did. Maybe that had to do with the fact that mom was black and dad wasn't. Or maybe it was the fact that I wasn't his dream son, he so desperately prayed for. Dad and I were close before mom left, but it was nothing like the bond mom and I shared. There were several times when mom had to go out of town for work and left me alone with dad to do my hair in the mornings for school. Those were the worst times, because I always went to school with terrible pig tails and a sore scalp. It was always easy with mom and a struggle with dad, because he didn't know how to work with the texture of my hair. I'm currently rinsing the cookie sheet I used for the garlic bread when I hear my dad's cell phone ring.

"What?" he snaps into the phone, causing me to slightly jump. I turn and look at him, but his back is towards me.

I can hear the person on the other end but I'm not able to make out the words. "Yeah, Yeah. I'm comin now Frank." he says sounding annoyed. He hangs up the phone and stands up while shoving the iPhone in his pocket.

"Looks like it's your luck day, Annabelle." he says as he leaves the kitchen. I watch as he grabs his keys that were on top of my red folder. He walks out of the door and when I hear it lock, I smile. I prefer to be home alone because he was only a constant reminder of how much my life sucks. Being in his presence, allows me to be vulnerable; it allows fear to settle within me. I despise that feeling but there's nothing I can do about it. I fix my plate and sit in my chair. I take a few bites of garlic bread as I began to reminisce once more about all the good times I've had in this room. I look up at the countertop spotting the orange mug that rests on top of the wooden breadbox. A mug with fancy black letters that spell out "MOM". That mug was bought by my dad and given to my mom on Mother's Day. During the first few years of her absence, I made it a habit to put her mug up there. I told myself I was doing her a solid, in case dad and I decided to rearrange some things in the kitchen. At least she would always be able to find her favorite mug. My eyes trail down the breadbox and find the burn spot on the white counter top. I shake my head and smile as I remember how the counter got that mark. It was the day of mom's birthday, that dad had the brilliant idea to make mom breakfast. That morning, we got up early to make pancakes, bacon, grits, and sausage. Everything was going smoothly up until grits were thrown into the equation. Dad was flipping the bacon when the grits started to pop. At this time, I was pouring orange juice in a glass cup that was on mom's food tray. The carton slipped from my hands and knocked over the glass, spilling orange juice everywhere. The glass then bounced off the tray, rolled off the table, and shattered as it hit the floor. Dad was putting the grits onto mom's plate when this happened. This caused him to place the pot on the counter near mom's plate as an immediate reaction. He rushed over to me and placed me on one of the chairs seeing as I was barefoot. He then began to sweep the shards of glass after inspecting me. He was in the midst of tossing the shards of glass in our green "glass only" bin, when it dawned on him that he left a hot pot on the counter. Mom wasn't too happy about that but she didn't exactly complain whilst eating her breakfast. It's the thought that counts. I take another bite of my garlic bread as I then make eye contact with my green hand print that stained the white pantry door. I remember that day like it was only yesterday. It was a birthday party my mom threw for me. After taking a community arts class, she thought it would be fun to have the kids paint a mural at my 5th birthday party. I was sitting at a wooden bench my dad put together for us in the backyard. My mom was standing over me watching as I smothered green paint onto the white paper. That was a grand day but it didn't stay grand for long because one of my best friends spilled blue paint on my dress. I smile a bit at how cute I thought he was yet mortified, that the paint would never come off my favorite yellow dress. Man, what was his name? I began going down a list of boy names in my head. After about two minutes of unsuccessfulness, I decide to give up. I eat the rest of my meal and wash my dish. Still standing at the sink, I look up at the blinds on the window in front me and see the small creamy tan colored curtain hanging in front of the blinds. It had brown seashells on it. Those were the curtains mom picked out for the kitchen the day we went to "TJ Maxx". My dad was opposed to the idea but he always caved when mom was involved. If only she left her secrets behind. I missed her so much. Tears began to form in my eyes. I glance over at the decorations and pictures mom put on the fridge. My eyes land on a picture in particular. It was framed in a red magnet in the shape of a square. This was the first picture we took together when we moved in. My dad had an arm wrapped around my mom's waist as he smiled at the camera. It's been a long time since I've seen the man smiling in this photo. I see a younger version of myself standing in the between them, with both my arms wrapped around each of their legs. I was smiling so hard that I'm surprised my face didn't fall off. My brown kinky, curly hair was up in one puff ball. The light from the sun that shone down on us, made my hair appear to be light brown. My mom had dark brown almond shaped eyes like mine and caramel colored skin. My dad had brown hair that was buzz cut and green eyes with stubble on his face. His white skin made him stick out as he stood next to mom and me. It was taken by my grandmother. She insisted that we stood by the oak tree that was in our front yard. She claimed it would definitely give off the family vibe. I shake my head and let out a puff of air as a smile makes its' way onto my face. Grandma was always funny. I swear she was a stand-up comedian back in her time. In the picture, we were all wearing jeans and a white shirt. If only that was us now. I hear the door open followed by my dad's loud voice.

"Yeah and next time it gives you trouble, please *do* interrupt me from eating dinner!" he says sarcastically. I turn around to see my dad sticking his head out the door as he talks to whoever is outside.

"You're a jerk! You know that William?" I hear the person shout back. "Jerk" isn't even the word I would use to describe this man. My dad laughs and shuts the door.

"Moron." he scoffs as he locks the door. He almost comes to a halt when he turns in my direction to see me watching him. It was like *I* startled *him*.

"That's a new one." I mentally think. He enters the kitchen and opens the fridge. With one hand on the top of the door he looks over at me.

"Shouldn't you be upstairs getting ready for bed?" he asks. I look down at the floor as fear starts to settle in. "I don't need to be late for work tomorrow." he says in a stern voice before leaving the kitchen with a beer in his hand. I take a deep breath before I make my way upstairs. I enter my dark room and close the door behind me. The light illuminating from the moon floods my room through the glass of the white double terrace doors. I walk onto the big white rug in the shape of a circle that's between my bed and the terrace. I really like this rug because it was soft like fur. I walk over to the terrace door and glance up at the full moon. I see the stars twinkling around it. There was a time where I thought I wanted to be a scientist. That is, until I took astronomy and had to memorize all the constellations. I sigh and turn towards my white twin bed. On the left side of my bed was the closet. It only held two pairs of shoes and a few clothes on the hangar. I didn't really have that many shoes or clothes for that matter. The only time I got the chance to buy something nice for myself is when I was granted money from *him* (and those times are very rare might I add). If there was one thing I did have, it was a lot of books. On the right side of my bed was a bookcase with six shelves. Some of those shelves had a few stuffed animals siting on the ledge. My mom bought that for me, once she discovered how much of a bookworm I was becoming. I walk over to my bed and plop down after setting the alarm that was on the night stand. Before I know it, I'm drifting off to sleep.

Chapter 2

"Picture perfect memories scattered all around the floor…" Lady Antebellum sang on the radio, as we drove down the long two-way road. The trees that were on both sides of the road made me feel like we were on a road trip (a scary one with all these trees). I didn't like this "back road" as my dad called it. Even though we were driving in broad daylight, I couldn't shake the thought of the creature from "Jeepers Creepers" jumping out to kill me. We didn't always take this route. Once my mom left, a lot of things changed. Before this, my parents always went through the neighborhood to get me to school. I like that way better because it was more friendlier and the view of our surroundings weren't blocked by trees. My paranoia isn't the only reason why I dislike this "back road". Taking this route meant it would take us some time to get to school. Especially on days when there was traffic. My thoughts were interrupted when my dad unexpectedly hit the steering wheel.

"Oh, come on!" he says in frustration. I look over at him just as he hits the steering wheel once more, making me flinch this time. We come to a stop as the white semi-truck in front of us stops. I look around the semi-truck, to see a long line of idle cars on the curved road ahead of us. I couldn't help the light smirk that forms on my face at the thought of me speaking too soon...opps...

"This is what happens when you're a jerk." I mentally think.

"I don't need this right now." He says with the same frustration in his voice. In the corner of my eye, I see him look in his rear-view mirror as his hand reaches for the gear shift. Was he going to attempt to turn around? My heart rate picks up and fear courses through me as the smirk I once held on my face dissolves.

"He can't even see around the vehicle in front of us but he's going to risk our lives just because he didn't want to be in traffic?" I mentally think, as I look over at him once more before looking in the side mirror near me. I see a red car on its way to get in line behind us. He curses and his hand retreats back to the steering wheel. I release the air I was holding, relieved that he didn't do what he was going to do. He was crazier than I thought. "I'm gonna be late for work and this is all your doing." He says while shaking his head with a frown on his face. It took about fifteen minutes before we were on the move again. When we arrive to our destination, he pulls up beside the sidewalk in the lane labeled "Buses Only". I look over at the time on his digital radio. I guess it's a good thing that school had already started. It was 8:30am. Great, I was six minutes late. I reach for my seat belt but stop once I feel his hand firmly grab my wrist, causing me to look into his green eyes.

"You don't have time for friends, or for boys, or for parties. You come to school to learn. You do your work and when school is over you come *straight*, home. Am I understood?" He asks in a deadly tone that I'm all too familiar with. I nod my head quickly and he lets go of my wrist. "Go on now." he says to me and I don't waste any time in helping myself out the car. He looked like he wanted to hurt me again. Thanks to him, I already have a big nasty bruise on my back from last week that still has some healing to do. When he drives off, I once again release the air held up in my lungs that I was unaware I'd been holding. I made my way to the double doors of the two-story, orange bricked building. "Terry Hills High school" was written in red letters across the top of the building. Just one more year after this one. I couldn't wait until graduation. I'd finally be able to get a job and eventually move out. I won't ever have to worry about seeing my dad's face ever again. I'll get out just like mom did and never come back.

"Hey! Annabelle!" I hear someone call out just as my hand touches the steel handle of the door. I look behind me to see three boys walking in my direction from the parking lot. I squint my eyes to see who it is (not like I have any friends here anyway), but they were too far away for me to make out any of their faces. They walked in a formation that put me in the mind of a gang. The boy who was calling out to me was in the middle and the other two guys were on the end. All three of them had their hands in their pockets as they walked in sync with each step. Getting an upsetting feeling about these people, I waste no time in pulling on the doors. The cool air from the inside brushes against my skin as I step inside. I walk as fast as I can. I pass a red bench on my right and it takes me back to my freshman year. Every day after school, my dad would sit on that bench waiting to take me home. I would pretend my mom was sitting there, reading her famous "Jet" magazine whilst waiting for me (I guess that's where I got my love for reading). I glance to my left as I pass by a dark blue hallway. I didn't like the fact that everything in that hallway matched because the dark color made it appear to be smaller than what it actually was. I see a few people present along with the echoing sounds of lockers opening and closing. I hope my classes aren't in that hallway. I continue down the giant orange main hallway, passing up a display of trophies won by our sports teams. There was also a display of our school's marching band uniform and other equipment such as a baton for the drum major. I make my way to the attendance office to get my schedule. I hear that same annoying bell jingle as I open the door. It was quiet except for the sound of someone typing on a keyboard. I was greeted with a white curved front desk. Sitting behind the desk, was a gray-haired lady I didn't recognize. She was wearing a red sweater over a white shirt with a collar. Anyone who sat in her spot was to page one of the attendance clerks when they had a student. She smiles once she notices me.

"Welcome back Annabelle! It sure is nice to see a lovely face." She says catching me off guard. How did she know who I was? "It *is* Annabelle, right?" she asks with a slight confused expression on her face. Maybe my face exhibited some confusion of its own that prompted her for reassurance. I smile and nod my head. "Okay, I was hoping I didn't mistake you for someone else. Mrs. Garcia gave me a description of you." She says as she presses a button on her keyboard. I understand Mrs. Garcia's reason for doing so, but it's not like I couldn't write to communicate. My "condition" (as I like to call it) wasn't *that* serious. "Mrs. Garcia is ready for you. This year, her office is in room 120. It's gonna be the last door on the right." the lady says interrupting my thoughts. I smile and advance to the hallway that's on the left side of the front desk. When I get to Mrs. Garcia's office, the first thing I notice was three stacks of yellow papers on her big rectangle shaped desk. She was currently taking a sip of her coffee while her eyes were glued to the computer screen in front of her. Her face lit up once her eyes connect with mine.

"Annabelle! It's so good to see you!" she says once she swallows. She puts the cup down and proceeds to dig through the stacks of schedules. She stopped all of a sudden. "Oh, I remember. I literally just printed your schedule off and stuck it in a folder over here for you." She said as she spun around in her green rolling office chair. She opened the bottom drawer of the black file cabinet that I hadn't noticed. Her dark burgundy hair that cascaded pass her shoulders, bounced as she moved around. She looked to be in her late forties. She wasn't skinny or fat. She was average. "Your first class is down the E wing. Good luck and if you have any concerns or questions don't be a stranger," she says as she takes my schedule out of the manila folder. "Most importantly, have a wonderful first day" she says as she hands me my schedule. I give her a nod as I return a smile of my own before walking out. I look at my schedule to see what classes I had this semester. I sigh when I see I have all the boring classes. I go to my first class and when I walk in, there's a male teacher talking to the class. I glance up at the circular clock hanging on the wall by the window. It was 8:45am. I couldn't believe it took me that long to grab my schedule. Everyone's attention went to me.

"...So, chemistry is all about knowing the behavior of atoms and their..." the teacher trails off as he realizes he wasn't the center of attention. He follows everyone's gaze and his eyes eventually land on me. He was sitting at a slight angle on the front of his desk. One of his legs were hanging higher than the other. He was dressed in black slacks, brown dress shoes, and a fitted dark royal blue shirt accompanied by a pocket on his left chest. He had curly black hair and brown eyes. He rubbed the facial hair that outlined his jaw. "Oh," he says with his British accent while smiling. I walk towards him returning a smile. "I'm Noel Wake but it's Mr. Wake to my students. And you are?" He says as he approaches me. He holds out his hand for me to shake it and introduce myself. Oh great, this again. I mean everyone should know of my "condition" by now. I hear a few whispers in the back of the room.

"Hey, isn't that mute girl!" someone shouts as if I were deaf. Half the class snickered and I got a few sympathetic looks from some of the other students. My eyes scan the snickering crowd, looking for the voice that spoke. My eyes finally land on a girl with brunette hair that was in a bun. She smirks devious at me as she mouths the word "mute" to me. I feel anger boil inside me. I was growing tired of being their laughing stock. I could only imagine what their faces would look like if I told them where they could stick it.

"She can't talk, Mr. Wake." A girl says. My attention shifts to her. Her name was Lori. We were study buddies for history in the fifth grade, before I was forced to push her away by my dad. She was Hispanic and had black hair with light brown eyes. I haven't seen her in a long time. She looked to be doing well. Still sitting in her seat, she turns around and faces the direction of the brunette. "And you, why don't you shut up and have some respect." she says to the brunette. The brunette scoffs at Lori.

"And maybe *you*, should mind your own business." She shoots back at Lori.

"You and your moron friends have picked on her for two years now. Just because she can't speak, doesn't mean she's stupid. Besides, even if she was, she'd still be a lot smarter than you will *ever* be." Lori replies back.

"OOO" the whole class says. The brunette stood up as an angry expression took upon her face. I was able to take in her appearance. She was wearing a black skirt and a white V-neck shirt that said "I don't care." in black letters. Let's just say her shirt matched her rotten attitude. On the other side of the room, a blonde girl with black glasses stood up abruptly. Her attention was on the brunette. She wore a jean jacket over an olive-green shirt and blue jeans.

"It's time to give it a rest Nina." the blonde girl said. Wow they must be high or something because no one ever stands up for me. I've always been the laughing stock.

"Yeah? And who's gonna make me?" Nina asks as she looks between Lori and the blonde girl.

"I will, if I have to." Lori says as she too was now standing.

"I'd love to see *both* of you try." Nina taunts as she rolls her neck and eyes.

"Hey! Hey! That's enough! Okay, quiet down. This is school, not a boxing ring. Sit down the lot of you!" Mr. Wake finally intervenes. The three girls stand still with their eyes glued to each-other.

"After you." Nina says in a harsh tone as she gestures to them. Lori and the blonde girl sit down reluctantly and Nina follows their lead. Nina's glare was still directed at the back of Lori's head. The room was filled with silence and tension until Mr. Wake spoke to me, telling me to sit anywhere I pleased. There were only two empty seats. One in the middle and the other in the very front, over by the window. I didn't even have to think much on it because if there was a seat up front, I would be in it. I make my way to the desk and quietly sit down.

"Now, as I was saying before..." he trails off as he walks back over to the desk to sit. I look out the window zoning out before I let out a sigh. Today was going to be a long tiring day. Once school was over, I retreat to my red locker to get my belongings. The hallway was empty, seeing as I was the last person (as usual). I put the last book in my back pack and when I closed my locker, I sensed a presence behind me. I turn around to an unfamiliar face.

"Hey." he says while smiling. Okay, what is happening? I give him a confused look. He obviously has the wrong person. Unless he's just being nice (which I highly doubt).

"I saw you while you were on your way inside. I...I didn't know you went here too." he says, sounding too happy for my liking. My eyes went side to side as I became more confused than I already was. "I was the one in the parking lot." he says letting out a nervous chuckle at the end. I feel my body slightly tense up as I feel afraid. What did he want with me? "You really don't remember me huh?" he asks sounding a bit disappointed as his smile slightly fell. "I'm Adam Vere, from fifth grade. W-we were best friends, before I moved away." he says, his eyes filling with hope. I stare at him for a moment. Adam Vere? Why did that sound so familiar to me...I gasp as the memories began to flood through my mind. Oh my gosh, Adam! I smile at him and nod my head. Without warning, he engulfs me in a hug. My body slightly tenses from the sudden contact. It's been a while since I've received a hug from someone. After a few seconds, my arms slowly find their way around him. I couldn't help the happiness I felt, because being in his presence always brought me joy. He was my childhood best friend after all. We've known each-other since kindergarten. We practically grew up together, with our families being close and all. We were almost like brother and sister until he gave me a strawberry flavored ring pop, the summer of fourth grade. That was the day he asked me to be his girlfriend. Being the naïve child that I was, (we both were) I said yes. He told me the ring was to represent a promise. A promise that he would always be there for me no matter what. From there, it went from writing letters and poems that did nothing but compliment me every day, to holding hands. I blush a bit as I think about that. I wonder if he still remembers those times. We had some great moments together, but that came to a halt when he moved away. He moved about two weeks before my mom left. It was certainly good to see him especially after all this time. We pull apart, still smiling at each-other. I use this chance to look at him. My eyes instantly travel down to his flashing teeth. They were always so white. Was that even natural? I move my eyes to observe his face. I see some of the features he had when he was younger. Like that one dimple on the left side of his cheek that could be missed by anyone when he smiled. Even though he didn't look too different from little Adam, I could also see some new features. He had grown some stubble on his chin, his jawline was more defined, and he wasn't a scrawny little kid anymore. That much was apparent from the fitted white shirt that showed the muscle of his arms. He stood at about 5'9 with brown hair that was parted on the right side. His eyes, warm, soft, and brown with hints of green swirling in them. Taking in his appearance, reminded me of why I found him attractive. I guess what people say is true. You're either born ugly and get cute or you're born cute and get ugly. Adam was never unattractive to me in fact, he was very attractive to me. His appearance wasn't the only thing that I liked about him. It was his personality. He was very caring, understanding, funny, and every time I was with him I was happy.

"Lookin good Annabelle, lookin good. How have you been? Like, what's going on? How's life treating you?" He asks, ambushing me with questions. I open my mouth to respond and as I do, I feel that familiar strain in my throat. I knew what was happening. I was suffocating. My chest becomes heavy as I start to panic. I lean on the lockers as my left hand went to my throat as it became impossible to breathe. I start gasping for air. "Oh my god." Adam says in a panicked tone. He looked terrified as he cried out for help. "Y-your'e gonna be okay. Alright?" he says trying to calm me down, but none of his strategies were working. I feel my knees give, out followed by the sensation of falling. "Annabelle!" I hear Adam yell as he lunges for me. He catches me before I could hit the floor. I almost close my eyes at the warmth I feel that radiates off of him as he holds me. I look at him just as I hear ringing in my ears. His head was turned to the left, as his lips moved. Everything that he was saying was indistinguishable. I didn't want to die here, especially in his arms. It wouldn't be fair to him if this was the last time he'd see me. Especially if it was because I made a stupid mistake. His worried face filled with concern looking down at me, was all I saw before everything was pitch black.

*   *   *

I couldn't open my eyes, but I knew I was on something incredibly soft. It couldn't be my bed because my bed was so rough, that you could literally feel the springs poking at your sides every time you moved. It couldn't even compete with this soft and comfortable material. "BEEP!" what was that? "BEEP!" I hear the sound of a door opening and closing.

"Is she going to be okay?" I hear my father's voice. It was filled with concern. Wait a minute, did *my* selfish, no good of a father just ask about *me* (Now *that's* a new one)? Whatever happened to me must've scared him because he's never concerned about me.

"The test we took came back normal, except her blood sugar. It is low which normally indicates that a person hasn't eaten. So, other than that, she is fine." I hear a male's deep voice say beside me. Low blood sugar? I was used to eating the bare minimum thanks to my dad. I shouldn't have passed out from that. This had to be another one of those vivid dreams I was having again.

"Thank god. I was really worried there for a minute." I hear my dad say sounding relieved. Okay, where are the cameras because I *know* he could care less if something happened to me. Unless…this was a wake-up call for him to appreciate my existence. The thought of having my dad back almost made me want to shed happy tears. It would take me a while to fully trust him again, given everything he put me through. Nonetheless, I would be more than willing to try if he was. I lost my mom and I've never felt so alone before. It would be nice if I could have *at least* one parent love me.

"I'm just gonna open the IV line and feed her the nutrients she needs. When she wakes up, I'll need to ask her a few questions and then she'll be free to go." the deep male voice said. I hear something click on the side of me. Wait, an IV? I was at a hospital? What happened? The sudden contact of something cold touching my arm made my eyes fly open, interrupting me from my thought process. The minute my eyes make contact with a white ceiling, they close on their own accord because of the brightness of the room. I open my eyes slowly this time and see the bright light above me. I look around the basic white room and spot my father with roses in his hand. He was sitting in a green and brown chair on the side of me.

Behind him were giant green curtains that blocked the window. I could see the orange light from the sun along the sides of the curtains. My eyes shift to the Tv hanging on the wall above the light brown door. It was on the news channel but no sound was coming from it. On the side of the door was a poster of the human body. I hear someone clear their throat and I slightly flinch as I see it was the doctor. He was adjusting the IV bag. He was a ginger and looked to be in his late twenties. I glance down at his white lab coat and see "Dr. David Kirk" engraved in blue letters on the right side. He looks over at me and smiles.

"Welcome back Ms. Wood." He says and I give me a nod with a light smile. He asks me a few yes or no questions regarding how I was feeling before he left me alone with my father. I look over at him the moment the door closes. My father after a while, places the flowers beside me on the small dresser. His eyes never meet mine like I was expecting them to. He then sits back down, still not making eye contact with me. I swallow as I began to feel anxious. He rubs the stubble on his jaw, as his green piercing meet mine. I knew that look all too well. He was angry (well, I can throw the "Having my dad back" wish out the window). I would never get him back because he enjoys the way he lives; hurting me. How could I have been so naïve to think that he would change? My eyes began to water a bit, as I feel sadness and anger settle.

He leans forward in the chair, resting his arms on his legs while lacing his hands together. He stays in that position for a moment, his eyes still on me. Right before I was going to look up at the ceiling, he spoke.

"The reason you're in here is because you tried to talk." he says in his usual harsh tone. Why would I do that? Who would *I* talk to? I search my mind for any possible reason as to why I would attempt such a dangerous thing. It was only then that an image of Adam's smiling face popped up in my mind. Adam...I saw him for the first time in forever. The anger and sadness that I once felt went away. I was glad he showed up when he did. I remember him greeting me in the hallway. The way he smiled at me and how happy I was to see him. That's why I talked, because he made me feel normal. I would have smiled if it weren't for my dad speaking again.

"I don't know if you're trying to do this whole "talking" thing again or what, but I *do* know, you weren't doing what I told you to do." He says in a low tone, not wanting his words to be heard. "I told you no friends, just school, and home. You go to school to learn, not to be friends with people." His voice became a bit louder as he spat at me in anger. His jaw flexed as he clenched his teeth. He took a deep breath; the one he would take when he was trying not to hurt me in public. My heart began to beat faster as fear and panic filled me. It didn't help that the heart monitor was giving away my secret. His eyes flickered to the monitor before settling back on me. Oh god, I've done it this time. There was a brief silence before he broke the spell. "If you don't follow my instructions, there will be consequences. And they won't just put you in a hospital. Am I understood?" He asks sounding a bit calm. I quickly nod my head. "Good." he says, emphasizing the word. He then leans back in the chair and closes his eyes.

Chapter 3

I sit silently in the car as I look out of the window on the way to school. I'm not even there yet and I'm already stressing because I know I'm behind in all of my classes. We pull up in front of the school and I get out and head towards the double doors. First period came and went. Second period came along and I had two thick packets of homework to catch up on. Why couldn't they have just given it to me in the hospital? I could have gotten a head start on the homework assignments. I couldn't have been happier when the lunch bell goes off. I make my way to my normal spot, outside under the oak tree. This tree was huge compared to me and it never failed to provide shade. I smile as I see that same blue jay bird standing on one of the branches. Its coat was a vibrant blue. It was so blue it almost didn't look real. They were always beautiful critters to me. I sit down and glance up at the bird to see it staring down at me. I smile and it cocks its' head to the side. This bird and I have been in each-other's company since freshman year (unless, it wasn't the same bird). My stomach growls reminding me of the yummy turkey sandwich I packed for lunch today. It had lettuce, tomato, mayo, and mustard on it. It was almost as good as mom's. I missed her so much and I wish it were my dad who left instead. I think life would have worked out best for me because I wouldn't have to deal with the things I deal with now. I close my eyes for a second and search my mind for a picture of her smiling face. When see I her, I smile and open my eyes. Sometimes just seeing her face in my mind helps to comfort me at times. I must've been in deep thought because I didn't notice Adam was crouched down beside me. He wipes a tear off my face and I flinch at the softness of his thumb. His eyebrows furrow as he looks at me.

"What's wrong?" he asks. I shake my head and try to mustard up a smile but I couldn't. "I was really worried about you. They wouldn't let me see you." he says as he sits next to me. I take out a piece of paper and pencil. I write to him, explaining to how over protective my dad is of me. I mean, he won't let me have any friends, or date so…that has to be some form of protectiveness. I'm not sure if that's because he's worried I'll get hurt or what. Even if that were true, he blew the mission because he's hurt me more than anyone. I was snapped out of my thoughts when Adam speaks.

"Why are you writing all this to me. I mean...why can't you just tell me?" he asks as confusion spread over his face. Oh dear, here we go again. I write to him explaining that I lost my ability to speak due to a traumatic experience. His expression went from confused to sad.

"Annabelle, I'm so sorry. I-I didn't know. I mean, I..." he trails off. I shook my hand and head to let him know it was okay as my eyes water. "When did this happen?" he asks. I couldn't stop the wave of sadness that hit me. I began to cry silently as dreadful memories flood my mind. They were too much. Before I knew it, I was in his arms. He cooed sweet things into my ear as I cried. I needed this. I needed someone to show me affection. My dad was a cruel man. He made me believe my mom's leaving was my fault. He said I should've been the one to leave. He wanted to give me up from the very beginning; not even *trying* to love me. Not even giving me a chance. My dad has treated me like crap for so long and the worst part is, I still love him...maybe he's right. I am pathetic and weak. The smell of Adam's cologne was calming me down a bit. I sniffle once more before pulling away from him. I give him a sad smile and he returns a comforting smile. I wipe my eyes. Great, now I have to go splash some water on my face to get rid of my red puffy eyes. Unless I want to walk around looking like I was crying (because that would be a good way to draw more attention to myself than needed). I stand up and he mimics my action.

"It's going to be okay Bee. We'll get through this together." he says trying to encourage me. Bee? I look at him surprised. He used to call me that when we were younger, and that was only because he couldn't get my full name right. It's been a long time since I was called that.

"I know it's been a while since we've seen each other but, I never forgot your all-time favorite nickname." he says while smiling. I couldn't help but smile back. There was something about his smile that lit a candle inside me. It was the type of smile one couldn't resist looking at and not throwing back a smile of their own. I look away as I feel my face heat up which results in Adam chuckling a bit. "Why Annabelle, are you blushing?" He teases while trying to sound as if he had a British accent. He laughs as I shake my head along with smiling. Then just like that, his facial expression changes. He looks at me with pure hate and disgust. My smile quickly fades as I feel a wave of rejection smack me in the face. I look at him again, and notice his hateful glare wasn't towards me, but at something behind me. I turn around to see a boy dressed in black jeans wearing a black leather jacket over his white shirt. As he got closer, I was able to see to see him clearer. He held a smirk on his face and his jet-black hair was slicked back. He reminded me of what we once called "greaser boys" back in the day. That instantly put me in the mind of the book I read in eighth grade called "The Outsiders". He slows to a stop, once he was a few inches from us. He was about the same height as Adam.

"Adam." He says in an Australian accent.

"Slade." Adam replies back in a harsh tone as he took a few steps in front of me. He did it in a way as if was trying to shield me, but why?

"It's nice weather we're having today, isn't it?" Slade says with a straight face that held no emotion. He then looks over at me and before flashing a flirty smile. I feel awkward as I watch his eyes look me up and down. Did he just openly check me out? "And who's this *fine*, piece of *hot?*" he asks, his eyes now on mine. Before I could even react, Adam struck Slade with his fist. Slade falls on the ground with a grunt. He stays in place as his hand goes to his nose. He pulls his hand away and chuckles before showing us the little blood that was on his hand. I was in total shock. "You hit softer than last time. You aren't going all girly on me, are you? If you are, that would be such a shame, seeing as I looked forward to this moment." Slade says with a smirk as he picks himself up. He wipes his nose with the back of his hand and chuckles once more, before he went for Adam without warning. I didn't know what to do. I couldn't yell for help and with the way they were fighting, I definitely did *not* want to get between these two. Slade tries to tackle Adam but fails once Adam latches onto him. He forcefully brings his knee up and it collides with Slade's chest. Slade grunts followed by few coughs. Adam then roughly shoves him, and this causes Slade to stumble. This gives Adam time to attempt the same move Slade tried to pull. The doors to the lunchroom open and two boys came out running. This made me jump because it was so sudden. I look back at Adam to see him on top of Slade throwing punches. I could only imagine how much it hurt because I could hear the contact every time Adam's fist collided with Slade's face. One of the boys had blonde hair, and the other had black hair. The black-haired boy went for Adam. I watch as he attempts to pull him off, but Adam pushes him back with one hand. Gosh, I knew guys were supposed to be strong, but not *this* strong. The boy went for him again and this time, he was able to get him off of Slade. Adam was raging with anger and his brown eyes were now a dark brown, almost black. My eyebrows furrow together as I look at them.

"Adam, you need to calm down right now man. Right, now!" the boy says while holding Adam, as if he would try to go after Slade again. He was breathing hard and he looked like he was straining himself. I could see the veins in his neck popping out. I hear a low animalistic growl that made the hairs on my neck stand up. Fear coursed through my body as I look around immediately hoping there wasn't some sort of animal finding its way towards us.

"No! Let go of me!" Adam yells, which turns my attention back to him. He struggles in attempt to get out of the boy's hold.

"Adam, you have to calm down. You're scaring Annabelle." I hear the boy tell Adam. How did he know my name? I've never seen any of these guys before. Adam slowly stops struggling. The angry expression was still on his face and if looks could kill, shoot I'd be dead on the spot. Before I could do anything, I hear a horrible noise that sounded hard enough to break through someone's skull. I look over to where Slade was to see the other boy's fist collide with his face.

"Don't you ever talk about her like that again!" the boy yells. I didn't know what was going on nor did I care. I just didn't want to be here. I feel everything but safe. I hear the bell ring, which meant lunch was over. It was time for 4th period. I quickly grab my things and race into the building. I was the first one to be in my seat. The teacher and I talked for a few minutes before everyone else showed up (or should I say, I just listened). After school, there was no sign of Adam, Slade, or the other guys who were with Adam. Since my dad worked tonight, I would have the whole house to myself. I didn't know where he worked but I prayed he worked every day so that I would only have to see his face in the mornings. I shut my locker and that's when I feel the presence of someone behind me. I slightly flinch as I came face to face with Slade. This was déjà vu all over again.

"Well hello, beautiful. I wasn't able to, *formally* introduce myself. I'm Slade, and you are?" he asks while flashing me that same flirty smile. I look at him to observe the damage that was done to him. His slicked back hair was a little ruffled. The bridge of his nose and the right side of his cheek were bruised. Seeing no reason in trying to flee, I stay quiet and look at the floor. I almost jump at the feel of his slightly cool finger lift my up chin so that we were both eye to eye.
"Beautiful? I didn't get that name." he says while looking at my lips as his hand retreats. My heart begins to pound in my chest.

"I thought I told you to leave her alone." I hear a very angry Adam say. I turn to see him standing a few feet down the hall. Slade smirks at me, not throwing a glance at Adam.

"He's always been a buzz kill." Slade says as he steps behind me. I feel his hot breath on my neck as he leans in towards my ear.

"See you around, beautiful." Slade whispers before walking off. I see Adam walking fast towards me, but his eyes were on Slade. That was a clear indication of what he wanted to do and I did not want to witness another fight. I step in front of him, grabbing his arm before he could pass me. His face was frowned and I could see his jaw flexing as he clenched his jaw. My touch must've caught him off guard because he snapped his attention to me. I gently let go of his arm and shake my head. His face softens as he sighs.

"Okay Bee. Okay." he says while nodding his head. "But just this once. Next time, I swear I'll..." he trails off while shaking his head.

"Did he hurt you?" he asks a few seconds later and I shake my head. "Did he touch you?" he asks. What? Why does that even matter? I've only seen Adam twice and we're just now I guess, "catching up". Why is he playing the protective card with me? Does he think he has to keep me from getting taken advantage of? Does he see me as fragile just because of my disability?

"Annabelle?" he presses interrupting me from my thoughts. Before I could answer him, he punches a locker. The sudden noise and movement makes me flinch. I begin to back away from him feeling a bit threatened. His eyes were that same dark brown, almost black color. His head snapped up at me. My eyebrows furrow as I try to get a better look. He closes his eyes turning away from me while taking a deep breath. "I'm sorry. I just, *really* don't like him." He says while turning around to face me. His eyes were the eyes I grew used to; brown, warm, and soft. "Slade and I have bad history. We've been at this ever since I moved. He likes to pick with everyone who I'm close to and he only does that because he knows it bothers me. He's toxic because none of his motives are good Annabelle. You saw how he was today...One day, I'll give him a taste of his own medicine." Adam says. I've never seen this side of him before. Something must've changed him because the Adam I knew, wouldn't even hurt a fly. I look at him and notice the angry expression that's written all over his face. I replay everything that happened today. The fighting and the rage I saw in him. He reminded me of my father. The look he had on his face was the look I always saw right before…

"Annabelle?" he asks with concern, pulling me from my thoughts. He was now closer than before. I smile and nod my head while trying to stop the tears from forming in my eyes. "Are…are you sure you're okay?" he asks. I could tell he noticed the tears forming in my eyes just by how he looked at me. I nod once more, grabbed his hand, and led him outside. "Woah there, Bee. I mean we only just reconnected a few days ago. I didn't know we were at second base already." He says as a smirk makes its way onto his face. I roll my eyes and let go of his hand. He chuckles in response. We walk at a steady pace, both of us silent before he spoke. "I'm sorry for what happened today. I-I'm not that kind of guy, and I don't want you to get the wrong impression. It's just today was already a bad day for me and he just amplified it. I saw how you looked at me today at lunch." He says while shoving his hands in his pockets. I look over at him to see the guilt on his face. "You looked scared of me Bee, and that's not what I want. I promise you, that I will find a better way to approach him whenever he bothers me. Violence isn't the answer, especially if it'll make your best friend afraid of you." he says. I give him a small smile and he returns his all-time famous smile that makes me smile even bigger. He chuckles. "There's that beautiful smile." He says as we get closer to the parking lot. We approach the bike racks that were stationed on the side of the steps you would have to walk on, upon entering the school. I slowly stop walking seeing as this is where we part our ways. He also stops once he notices I'm no longer walking next to him. He throws me a look, as if to say "What are you doing?" I point in the direction I walk to get home

"You *walk* home?" He asks almost in disbelief. I nod and give him a small smile with a wave and begin my journey. "Wait." he calls out. I stop and turn around. "You don't have to walk, you know. Let me give you a ride home." he offers as he approaches me. As much as I'd like that, I can't risk being seen with him. Especially not after my last little episode. I shake my head as I began to walk. He walks beside me. "Why would you wanna do that? It's about to rain," he says while looking up at the clouds. "You wouldn't wanna walk in the rain, now would you?" he asks trying to persuade me. I look up and sure enough it was super cloudy. How could I have not noticed this. I'm usually on point about the weather. I guess I better walk faster if I want to make it home in time. I just need to pay attention next time. A sudden loud boom that sounded from the sky accompanied by the cloudy gray clouds, made me jump. Adam chuckled a bit while looking at me. Me being startled tickled him?

"Look, just wait here and I'll bring the car around." He says as he tosses me his super light black backpack. He takes off jogging before I could do anything else. Well, so much for walking home. I mean I'm not complaining. I'd rather come home dry instead of having my books soaked. The faster I get home, the faster I can eat. I turn around fast as I hear someone scream.

"Josh, stop!" a girl says to a boy who had men's cologne in his hand, stalking towards her. There were a lot of people outside, but most were gathered in crowds loading the buses. A few boys were skating and doing tricks and some were throwing a football back and forth.

"Hey, *mute!*" I hear a familiar feminine voice call out. I turn around only to see something flying towards my face. I didn't have time to make out what it was because I was suddenly yanked back only to be facing someone's back. It was Adam. I hear the familiar voice scoff.

"What is up with everyone sticking up for that, *thing?* I thought you knew better than that! She's so below us. Why is that so hard for everyone to see?!" the feminine voice says in frustration.

"The only difference between you and her, is that she doesn't have to stoop so low to get people to like her. Unlike you, she's pretty awesome—"

I hear the girl cut him off with a scoff.

"Awesome? Who said that? How would *you* even know? You *just* got here. Nobody talks to this half and half mute. She doesn't even like herself? I mean really, look at her." the feminine voice says. Adam tells her to stop throwing her insecurities off on me in a stern voice that reminds me of my father. Before the girl could reply, Mr. Wake's voice pierces through the crowd.

"Did I miss something? Was I not invited to the party we're having out here? School is out, let's gooo! Clear the area! If you're waiting for the buses, you know where to go. Everyone else, clear out!" The crowd quickly disperses while I step from behind Adam to see who that familiar voice belonged to. This girl was Margareta, but she went by Margie. She was about 5'2 height wise. She was thick in a sense that she was constantly active in sports. Her skin was almost pale, as if she didn't believe in being in the sun. She had red hair, freckles on her checks, and always wore red lipstick to match her hair color. We've been going to the same school since kindergarten, and she never liked me. I never knew why or what I ever did to make her hate me so much. This wasn't the first unfriendly encounter I've had with her. Her words never got to me, especially seeing by now I'm used to her pettiness. I've learned to just block out the negativity that emits off her. When Margie's eyes catch mine, she throws me a glare before she imitates the fleeing crowd. I look at Adam as he turns to face me. My eyes go down to the chocolate pudding that was smashed on his chest. I couldn't believe he just took a hit for me. How did he get here so fast? I mean he had just left, right?

"I know what you're thinking and because I do, don't thank me. This is what best friends do. Plus, Margie is Margie. Next time, I'll bring the pudding, you throw it, and I'll take the blame for it. I promise." He says while chuckling. I smile and shake my head. I look up as I hear the sound of rolling thunder. Within seconds, I feel little cold rain droplets hit my face.

"Come on." he says as he takes my hand and leads me to his black mustang. "Welcome to what I like to call "The Bat Mobile". He says as he opens the passenger side for me. I smile and get in. A few seconds went by (too long if you ask me) before he got in the car. I was beginning to wonder what was going on but when he got in the car without a shirt on, my question was answered. He tossed his white chocolate pudding ruined shirt in the back. I look over at him.

"This isn't gonna be a problem for you, is it?" he asks, gesturing to his abs as a smirk appears on his face. I quickly avert my gaze and stare straight forward, as I feel myself blushing. He laughs as he put the car in drive. The ride home was silent but awkward. When he pulls in my driveway he gets out and opens the door for me while shielding me from the rain with his ruined shirt.

"I know it's not an ideal umbrella but I'd take a chocolate pudding ruined shirt umbrella any day." He says while chuckling which causes me to smile. He walks me to my porch while shielding me from the rain.

"See you tomorrow Annabelle Wood." he says while walking backwards. I smile and wave before closing the door. I lean my back against the door smiling, but the faint smell of alcohol reminds me of where I am. This causes my smile to fade. Thank God, my dad wasn't home. I would definitely get it if he spotted Adam outside our house, and it wouldn't help if he was seen without a shirt on. I let the back of my head rest on the door with my eyes shut as I sighed. Tonight, would definitely be a long one. I wipe my wet feet on the dark green mat that said "Welcome Home" in faded black letters. I walk pass the stairs and into the kitchen. I decide to look for something to munch on as I do my homework. I approach the refrigerator and my eyes land on the picture of my parents. They were both teenagers in this photo. My dad stood behind my mom with his hands wrapped around her waist. My mom's hands rested on my dad's hand as they both smiled brightly at the camera. I notice the red and white "Dairy Queen" sign in the background that was cut off between the two "e's". That was their favorite place to go and eventually it soon became mine. It's been too long since I've been to a "Dairy Queen". I smile at how happy they look. The smoke detector beeps, indicating that the batteries need to be changed. This snaps me out of my remising moment. I approach the white linen cabinet door. I open it and grab my Nutella and a pack of club crackers (don't judge). I proceed to my room and start on my homework until the alarm I always set for myself to make dinner does off. I didn't get to eat until my dad got home but that didn't stop me from sneaking a few strips of grilled chicken. I was currently cutting a few slices of cucumber for the grilled chicken salad when the phone rang. I answer it and was greeted by my dad's voice.

"Good, you're home." My dad says sounding almost as if he didn't want me to be. Although I was used to this kind of treatment, I couldn't help feeling a bit hurt by this. "You can go ahead and eat dinner. I won't be home for a week. Remember what I said. No friends. No nothing. Just school and home." And with that, he hangs up. I smile because I was gonna eat good tonight.

Chapter 4

I'm standing in a familiar forest with my back to a cliff. In front of me stood a forest. I see the familiar shadows emerging from the trees. They appeared to be people. What's going on? The scene before me slowly changed. I look around confused seeing I was no longer in a dark scary forest. The moon was replaced by a beautiful orange sky, indicating that the sun was trying to rise. I flinch as I see a bald man standing in front of me along with a huge crowd of people. The bald man was dressed in a brown robe. We were still in what looked like a forest, except this forest was a lot friendlier than the one I was currently in. All the trees had orange and red leaves. The grass was a healthy green color. It almost didn't look real. The warm breeze brushed up against my skin.

"You are a disgrace to this family! You have tainted yourself in filth, compromised your brothers and sisters, and worst of all, you turned members of this family against each-other! You have been a disgrace not only to me as your father, but also to the queen of this community! We will no longer tolerate your existence." the man says as his angry and hateful glare cuts through me.

"Hansel, please!" I beg, but it wasn't my voice.

"No! You have begged your way too much! We have shown great mercy to you. I'm afraid you have run out of chances, my dear Tabitha." Hansel says with no type of sympathy. Tabitha? I try to speak but no words come out. I try to move but it was like I wasn't...me. I've had dreams like this before but this...this was different. I look amongst the crowd and my heart is pricked with sadness and shock as I spot my mother. She was dressed in a robe like everyone else. The only difference was the color. She was in a white robe with red tribal markings. I watch as she pulls her hood off. She was watching the scene like everyone else. She had a sad expression on her face that told how sorry she felt for you. I desperately try to move to reach my mom but I was stuck, frozen. A man steps from the crowd. He approaches me and cups the side of my face. His blue eyes look into mine as a sad expression takes upon his face.

"My beloved, don't let them do this to me. To us, please." Tabitha pleads.

"I'm sorry, my beloved. If you have committed these treacherous things that you are being charged with...I...I cannot be with such a woman." the man says. He pulls away and walks back to join the crowd. Tabitha began to protest but was cut off by Hansel.

"You have violated the family code and it is well known, what punishment lies ahead." Hansel turns to face the crowd. "Mark my words, if any rule shall be broken, execution will be the result!" Hansel warns the crowd.

"No! Please, I...I had a good reason. Nick, he...he needed our help. He—" Tabitha began to say but was cut off by Hansel speaking a native language that I've never heard before.

"Wait!" Someone from the crowd calls out. A woman approaches me with a sad expression. This woman looked vaguely familiar. She was dressed in a black robe and over her head she wore a gold hood. I wasn't able to see her face until she took off her hood. She was Asian with brown eyes and straight black hair.

"You came." Tabitha says with a mixture of happiness and surprise as the woman embraced her. I couldn't feel the hug. She pulls back and her mouth begins to move but I can't hear what she's saying. I hear a familiar muffled sound. It almost sounded like a something was beeping. Everything became blurry and the sound became clearer and louder. I jolt awake at my loud alarm going off. I groan as I reach over and turn it off. I hate when my alarm finds a way to incorporate itself into my dreams. This was the second time I had this dream. Why was I having these vivid dreams now? I used to have a lot of vivid dreams when my mom left and those weren't good dreams. Every time I had one, I always woke up with a panic attack. My dad who wasn't nearly as cold as he is now, took me to the doctors and they explained that stress was triggering it. I guess the recent events that were happening between Adam and Slade were causing me to stress (and let's not forget my dad). I decide to lay still for a few seconds to allow my breathing to go back to normal. I sit up a bit surprised as I realized my dad didn't shout for me to get ready. A smile works its way on my face as it dawns on me that he's not home. He wouldn't be for a week. I gracefully make my way to the bathroom and take my time showering. I even make an effort to hum a little tune mom would hum to me before tucking me in for the night. Once I get dressed, I brush my wet, curly, and wavy hair into a bun. I make my way downstairs. The house was quiet except for the creaking of the first few steps. I love it when the house is this quiet. We were both free of my dad's presence. I make my way into the kitchen and grab my lunch. I head out the door making sure to lock it and start my journey. It was a pretty good distance but I'm not complaining, because it feels good not to be terrified of him wanting to hurt me because I didn't cook his bacon the way mom would. I miss her so much and I wish that she would've taken me with her. I walk two blocks from home and I so desperately wanted to crawl on the ground or lay in someone's lawn. I had a long way to go and the hot sun beaming down on me wasn't helping. An unfamiliar mustang slowly cruised on the left side of me. Fear begins to course through me as I think this could potentially be a kidnapping. I pick up my pace and walk faster as my heart pounds in my chest. The mustang matched my pace. I hear the window roll down. Oh god, this is it.

"You want a ride?" a familiar voice yells out. I stop and bend down a bit to look into the car and relief washes over me when I see it was Adam. "Sorry for the whole, creepy stalker cruise thing I had going on. I thought it would make me look cool." he says jokingly. He leans over and opens the door for me. I couldn't help the smile that forms on my face as I get in. When we get to school, I catch quite a few jealous glares from some of the girls. He holds the door open for me and we proceed to our classes. I was currently sitting in geometry learning about properties of similar triangles when the door opens. Ms. Washburn, our principal enters. She was a skinny African American with straight black hair. She was wearing a dark navy skirt with a blazer to match and black flat shoes. She approaches Mrs. Nicks who was her twin. They were spitting images of each-other except Mrs. Nicks had a curly afro. She was dressed in a grey blazer with pants to match and a red shirt underneath.

"Good morning sis." Ms. Washburn greets Mrs. Nicks.

"And to what do I owe this pleasure." Mrs. Nicks replies with a smile.

"Well, you have a new student today." Ms. Washburn says and then turns her attention to the class.

"Good morning," she greets the class. "We have a new exchanged student from Australia. Please make him feel welcome in our wonderful school." She says with a smile on her face. She nods to whoever was in the hallway and they walk in. No. Freaking. Way. It was Slade. I thought he already went here. He probably wasn't supposed to be here yesterday. "Have a great day, Slade." Ms. Washburn says to him right before she walks out. His eyes scan the room and stop once they land on me. He smirks a little. Oh gosh.

"Slade, you may sit wherever you'd like. But be mindful that these seats *are* permanent unless I see reason to change them. So, pick carefully." Ms. Nicks says to him. There were two empty desks on the side of me. Why couldn't there have been someone sitting next to me? He looks between me and the closets desk to me. The smirk on his face becomes more present as he approaches the desk next to me. He sits down and to my surprise, he doesn't utter a word. Half of class went by smoothly and I was quite surprised to be honest. I was expecting Slade to be "toxic" as Adam put it but so far, he was showing his good side. I was just finishing my homework, when a piece of paper appears on the right side of my desk. I open it and read it.

"I still didn't get that name beautiful." It read. I might have spoken too soon. I shake my head. Will this guy leave me alone already? I write back to him telling him to leave me alone. He chuckles. He makes me very uncomfortable, especially now that I know he only sees me as a "fine piece of hot".

"Playing hard to get I see?" he says as he writes something on the paper before handing it to me. He stands up just as the bell rings. I look at the paper to see he wrote his number. When I look back up to scold at him, he was gone. I roll my eyes and throw it into the trash on my way out. I didn't want this to turn into a flirt fest for him. I go to my next class and was able to breathe when I discovered it was Slade free. Thank the Lord. Adam was in here and I could feel his gaze on me the entire time. This too was making me uncomfortable. I escape Slade trying to moon me only to come here as something to stare at. I couldn't seem to catch a break. This was overwhelming. I couldn't focus at all because I was too distracted by him. When the bell rings, I waste no time in being the first one out. At least they won't bother me today because I won't be in my usual spot. I'll be in the library. The library was one of the biggest rooms in the school. It was two floors. I make my way to the library and I take a deep breath as I see many students entering. The aroma of bagels and cinnamon fills my senses. I look up to the second floor through the glass railing and see a few students lined up by the bistro. I decide to take the second floor. There were a few students looking at books and a few librarians walking around supervising the students.

"Unfortunately. It's so obvious she's desperate, I mean really. Why else would she allow herself to be that reckless? I couldn't imagine that being *me*, like what even." I hear Margie say. I turn in the direction of her voice to find her sitting with two other girls. One of them was Nina. She was on her phone texting while smiling. The other brown-haired girl shook her head as if to say "What a shame". as she was listening to Margie. I roll my eyes as I pass by them.

The aroma of bagels and cinnamon only becomes stronger as I walk up the stairs. I see a few empty tables. I spot one all the way in the back and decide to stake my claim. If they do come looking for me there's a great chance they won't find me thanks to the many bodies that are occupying the table in front of me. They all seemed to be playing a game online together with their Nintendo's. For good measure, I sit with my back facing the only direction you can approach this table. That way, if they see the back of my head they might assume I'm not their target. I pull out my lunch and open my favorite book. I was so excited to read it because it was just getting to the good part. The main character, "Star" had just tasted human blood for the first time in four hundred years. I continue to read for a while as I take small bites of my turkey sandwich. I take a sip of water and I suddenly get this paranoid feeling. The hairs on my neck stick up as I feel as though I'm being watched. I turn around to see a smaller line for the bistro. The table of gamers were still present. My eyes scan amongst the many students in here. Two people were arm wrestling, two guys were playing chess a few tables down from me, and the majority of the population was conversing quietly. I turn around only to gasp while putting a hand over my heart as I see Slade sitting in the other chair across the table. How in the world did he manage to sneak up on me like that?

"Well, that's the only sound I've ever heard you make." he says while chuckling.

"Go away please." I write on a piece of paper that was at the table when I first sat down. He looks at me.

"You don't talk much, do you?" he says sounding a bit disappointed. Was he serious? I mean I know he's new and all, but I know someone's mentioned my status to him by now. "The mute freak", Annabelle Wood. Everyone in this school knew about me and my "condition". I write to him explaining that I couldn't talk due to an accident that happened a few years ago. After reading the paper, his face was wiped clean from his little smirk and replaced with sadness.

"Oh, I'm sorry." he says. A few seconds pass by before he speaks again. "If you need anything," he leans across the table "and I mean anything, I'm your guy. Oh, and I will get that beautiful name of yours." he says with a wink as he gets up and walks away. Finally, I get to have some peace and quiet. I watch as he approaches another girl standing in line for food. I roll my eyes. I wasn't too fond of guys like him. I turn my attention back to my book, hoping to get back into the story until the bell rings. Are you kidding me? Whenever I actually *want* to read, I can't. If it's not school, it's something at home. I scoff as I gather my things and exit the library. Afterschool, I grab my things out of my locker and start for the door when my name was called. I turn around to see Adam jogging towards me.

"Hey," he says smiling. I smile back. "Um, don't get mad or anything okay?" he says nervously. I give him confused look. "Remember when you told me you couldn't talk?" he asks and I nod my head and urge him to continue. "Well I was thinking, and well, maybe you *could* get your voice back." he says. Was he joking? Please tell me he's joking because I haven't spoken since the day my mom left. Don't think I haven't tried because I have. The only problem is every time I attempt; it ends in me fighting to breathe. Some things you can do in life and others you can't. Speaking is one of those things that fall into the category of "Impossible". I was brought back to the incident I had here recently. I shake my head. I didn't want that for myself.

"You don't wanna talk anymore?" he asks. I flip to a clean page in my blue notebook.

"You don't understand." I write to him. He looks at me with his eyebrow furrow together.

"Then make me understand. Annabelle, I'm your friend and I know I haven't always been around but I want nothing but the best for you." he says. That was sweet of him but I'm far from being helped. I shake my head once more and make my way to the front door. I feel the wind hit me as I push open the door. "You don't wanna be helped? Is that it?" he asks keeping up with my pace. "Or is it because you're afraid?" he asks causing me to stop. He mimics my move and looks at me. The truth is, I am afraid. I'm afraid that if I talk I'll die. I always end up reaching for air, as if it can save me. I come close to death and that is what scares me the most. He doesn't understand. If I had a chance of being helped, doesn't he think I would've taken that opportunity already? And why is this so important to him? Why can't he just leave me alone? "You could use my help and-" I cut him off by putting my hand up and walking away. I was beginning to get upset with the fact that he was so persistent about this talking thing. I gave him my answer, so why couldn't he just drop it? "So that's it then? You're just gonna check out on me because you're afraid?" he questions but I keep walking and he doesn't follow me this time. I can finally have some time to think by myself. It was only Monday and things were already spiraling out of control. You know what I need? A hot, steaming shower. That for sure will calm me. Getting home, I throw my back pack on the floor in my room and head straight to the shower. The hot soothing water cascades down my body, touching my bruises. I love the aftermath of a hot shower. It always helps to loosen my tense muscles. When I get out, I do a double take at the clock on my nightstand. It was five o'clock. I got home around three. I've been in here for almost two hours. Man, I'm really losing it. I brush my wet hair out and make sure to put detangling spray in my hair to assist me with brushing it out. This was something I always struggled with, especially seeing that I have what my mom always said "A head full of hair". I smile a bit as I think of all the times she helped me brush my hair out after a shower. Now I'm doing it alone. Once I brush my hair out, I put my curly and wavy hair into a wet bun. This was the process every time for me. I then brush my teeth and when I'm finished I do my homework. When I complete the assignments, I put everything in my backpack and decide to treat myself to some entertainment. This led me to catch up on my show "American Horror Story" in my dad's beer infested room, since I didn't have a Tv of my own.

Chapter 5

Adam ran fast through the woods dodging tree by tree, with a cut on his bare back and blood on his torso.

"He's straight ahead!" a voice calls out from behind him. They were hot on his trail and wanted him dead. He quickly climbs high up a tree and watches as three men with guns run pass him. He climbs down after a while and runs in the opposite direction. He winced in pain with each breathe he took. His bare feet crushing the dead leaves on the ground as he ran for his life. His light blue jeans were stained in a mixture of dirt and blood. He slows to stop as he approaches a hill. He bends over as he tries to catch his breath. The sound of a twig snapping makes him stand up straight as he looks in the direction it came from. His mouth was slightly open as he breathed hard. Right before he could take off, a gun goes off. He cries out in pain as the bullet hits him. The impact was so hard that it made him fall and tumble down the hill he was on. The man who shot him quickly approaches the hill with the silver pistol in his hand. He was dressed in a black leather jacket and blue jeans. The shadows of the trees created by the moon, hid the man's face. The green laser on his gun cuts through the darkness as he points his gun down the slope of the hill. Adam was nowhere to be found.

"The target was hit but I can't confirm the kill. I'm east of where we set the traps. Rendezvous my position and we'll search the area and neutralize the threat. It won't make much ground, at least with the bullet I put in him." the man says as with one finger pressed onto the earpiece in his right ear. I jump up, awakened by the vivid dream I was just having. I was breathing hard and beads of sweat covered my forehead. I'm greeted by darkness, which isn't normal for my room. It was never dark in my room. I look around the room and see a red light emitting from an alarm clock I didn't recognize. It said, "2:15 am". Where was I? I get up, swinging my legs over the bed I was on. Where was I? I slowly stand up and take a small step forward. My bare foot touches something cold. I retract my foot back from the sudden contact and my foot knocks something over. It isn't until I hear the sound of glass bumping into each-other that realization settles in. I fell asleep in my parent's room. I quickly find my way out. I walk down the white hallway until I reach my room. I get into my bed and lay down. Good thing my dad didn't decide to show up...I could only imagine what would happen. I stare up at the semi-lit ceiling (thanks to my terrace) and reminisce about the dream I just had. Why was I dreaming about Adam being chased down and shot? I didn't want to dream about him getting hurt. Sadness began to settle in at the thought of something bad happening to him. If anything, I should be having happy dreams about him, because that was the only thing he brought me.

Chapter 6

Two weeks have passed and I haven't seen Adam at all. I was currently in geometry trying to listen to the teacher lecture about the lesson, but it seemed impossible. I couldn't shake the feeling that something bad might have happened to Adam. Thinking back to the dream I recently had, wasn't helping my case at all. What if I had a premonition? What if he was shot last night?

"Any questions?" I hear the teacher ask, pulling me out of my concerns. I look around the room and no one says anything. Great, now I have no idea what we're doing. I look around at everyone else and see them working on the homework packet for the week. I mimic them.

"Just focus on what you're doing." I mentally tell myself as I open the homework packet. I guess this was a good idea to get a head start on the homework. Slade thought otherwise because he was talking every five seconds. He kept asking me for my name and what I had planned for the weekend. It's like he's obsessed with me for whatever reason. There's not much to my story. My mom walked out on us, leaving me with my abusive father who beats me every time I do something "wrong". What's so interesting about *that?* For two weeks, it's been him and me. The bell rings and I rush out trying to avoid Slade. I even tried eating my lunch in my chemistry class during the tutoring hours available in that time frame, but nope. He still found me. He said he was "finishing" a test that he didn't have time to complete, but I didn't buy it. It didn't help that every time I looked up, he was watching me. I couldn't get rid of him. Lost in my thoughts, I bump into a wall which results in me dropping my books. Nice one Annabelle. Way to make yourself look more like a freak. I then notice it was a person when I heard a familiar male voice apologize. It was him, Adam. Thank god, he's okay. I don't think I've ever been this happy to see Adam. He helps me pick up my belongings and I take out a piece of paper out of my green binder.

"Where were you? You had me worried something might have happened to you." I write to him. After reading the paper he smirks and looks up at me.

"You totally missed me." He says. I roll my eyes and he chuckles. I was just glad he was okay. Just then, Slade comes out of our recent class calling after me. Oh great, just my luck. Slade's facial expression fills with disgust and pure hate as he notices Adam standing next to me.

"Adam." He says.

"Slade." Adam hisses back in annoyance. I look down at Slade's hand and notice he has my favorite book. I must've forgotten it was under my desk.

"What do you want?" Adam asks harshly.

"I came here for her, actually." Slade replies before turning his attention to me. "You left this behind." He says as he hands the book to me. He then looks at Adam for a brief moment before walking away. Adam watches him until he turns the corner.

"I am going to punch that stup-" I touch his arm making him stop his sentence. He must've been caught off guard because his eyes snap to mine. His angered face softens a bit when his eyes lock with mine.

"I'm sorry. I know I promised no violence but it's just I...one of these days, someone is going to knock him flat." He says. Adam and I walk over to my normal spot for lunch. I listen to talk about his cousin's wedding he attended for the time he wasn't here. He said there was a chocolate fountain which I would love. They all went canoeing as a family as an after party. It sounded like fun. I'm surprised I even remember that word. Thankfully after lunch, the rest of the day was peaceful. I was currently walking out the doors of the school when I hear Adam calling my name. He catches up to me by running.

"Hey, I was thinking that I might have taken the wrong approach. I want to know if you want my help?" he asks nervously. Want his help? With what? I give him a confused look.

"Helping you talk, is what I mean." he says. I shake my head. I'm not doing this again. I take out a piece of paper from my planner.

"Why can't you just drop it? If you don't like how I 'am, then just leave me alone. Just join the idiots who mock me. I think it would be best if you did." I write and with that, I push the note into his chest. I storm off not giving him a chance to read it. Clearly, he's not my friend. He's not the Adam I once knew. If he were, he'd accept me the way I am, wouldn't try to change me for his likings.

Chapter 7

Ugh! I have to walk to the grocery store to get ingredients for some yummy lasagna. I need some rosemary, butter, and tomato sauce to make it just the way mom would. I don't fancy the idea of going out this late but I didn't have a choice, seeing as there was nothing for me to eat. I check the pantry for a least some cereal or canned food. I was out of luck. I grab my house keys, really wishing they were keys to a car and make my way outside. The neighborhood was peaceful but the walk was...scary. It was dark and so foggy that if someone were walking a few feet in front of you, you wouldn't see them until after you bumped into them. I couldn't shake the paranoid feeling I was getting. The hairs on my neck pricked up for the entire dreadful walk. I let out a sigh of relief once I make it inside "Terry's Grocery Store". I'm greeted with the sound of the cashiers ringing customers up as I grab one of the mini red shopping basket that was stacked in a pile. I look around with my eyes to find the store had changed since the last time I was in here. The bread section on the left was replaced by the produce and a bakery section. Across from that section were clothes. This store put me in the mind of Wal-Mart because of the way it was set up. I start my journey to fetch the ingredients. Everything was going smooth until I went to get the butter. Out of the corner of my eye, I see someone looking at me. I slowly look over to the person to see their attention was on the cheese that was in front of them. They casually grab a pack of cheese. This person looked to be a man but I couldn't see his face because he was wearing a black hood. Maybe I was just being my normal paranoid self. I grab the butter and let out a breath when I see the man walk away from the cheese section. I just need to get the tomato sauce and get out of here. When I get to the aisle for the tomato sauce, it takes me a while to find the right one. I wasn't a fan of mushrooms but that was the one mom used that made the lasagna so delicious. My grip on the black handles of the basket tighten as I feel like someone's watching me. Once again out of the corner of my eye, I see the same person. He walks at a slow pace down the aisle. My heart starts to race.

"He's not following you. He's shopping just like everyone else." I mentally tell myself. Not thinking about it, I grab whatever tomato sauce is in front of me and I walk a fast pace out of the aisle. I need to get the cash register. As I pass by the aisles I gasp as I see that same man standing still with his back to me. He *was* following me. I wasn't just being paranoid. I break out into a jog as fear fills my body. My jog was cut short once I bump into someone. They let out a little shriek as they stumble back a bit. "What is your prob—" the person stops short once their eyes meet mine. It was none other than Margie. She scoffs and her face scrunches up in disgust, as she looks me up and down.

"What are you, blind too? Watch where you're going, mute. It would be such a shame for you get hurt because you're not paying attention." she says in an annoyed tone. She then rolls her eyes and walks off. She was the last person I wanted to see. I look around me in search for that man but he was nowhere in sight. I hurry to the cash register, pay for my items, and head to the exit doors. Holding the grocery bag in one hand, I approach the automatic doors. When they open, I say a quick prayer to god that I'd make it home in one piece. I step out the store and began my walk home. Jeez, I thought walking to the store was scary. Having to walk pass all these creepy dark alleys was the main concern for me walking in the first place. You never know what could happen. As if on cue, someone pulls me into an alley. I'm roughly pushed up against the side of the building. Pain shoots up my spine as the hard brick wall makes contact with my nearly healed back. My heart pounds rapidly in my chest as I try to break free from the man who grabbed me. I couldn't speak nor could I call for help. I was completely vulnerable because not only was there one guy, but two. He pins me harder into the brick wall and wraps his hand around my neck.

"I wouldn't bother trying to run, little lady." the man says as he roughly grabs my hair, making me look up at the dark sky. All I could do was sob silently and let the tears fall where they may. He let go once he notices I was crying and wipes the tears off my face before his hand went back to my neck.

"Don't worry. I'm gonna take *real* good care of you, sweet pea." He says as he pushes himself onto me. I was totally trapped between him and the brick wall. My heart rate increases as I feel his hot breath on my neck. They both wore grey dirty sweatpants and a leather jacket.

The only difference was that the other man wore a beanie. The man who grabbed me tosses my purse with his free hand, to the other man who was looking through the groceries that flew out my hand when I was grabbed.

He smirks and strokes the side of my face as I cringe under his touch, instantly feeling the need to take a shower. He puts his head in the crook on my neck and I flinch from the sudden movement.

"Hm. You smell good." He mumbles against my skin. I squeeze my eyes shut, feeling myself shake as tears continue to fall down my face. God, please take me now. I don't want to die like this.

"Ian, stop scaring the poor girl." I hear the other man say as he continues to go through my purse. Ian pulls back from me and I open my eyes and look at him.

"It's fun this way, otherwise why do it right?" Ian says as his eyes go to my lips. Oh god, please no. He leans in and instead of doing what I thought he was set out to do, he searches my jacket pockets. He digs out my keys, a receipt from the store, and a pack of juicy fruit gum.

"She's got nothing." he says in disappointment as he returns the items back into my pocket.

"Yeah, you're right. No credit card, no ID...no nothing. But we'll take the cash." the other man says. He smiles at me before putting the cash in his pocket. His facial expression was now serious.

"Dispose of her, and then we can get out of here." the man says as he continues searching my purse. Ian pulls out a gun and cocks it back. I saw my life flash before me. I saw how both my parents and I were happy before all this started. I hear a loud animalistic growl which causes me to look around. Ian must've heard it too because he swung in the direction in which it came from with the gun shaking in his hand. The other guy didn't seem to hear it because he was too busy going through my purse. I had a lot of stuff in there. I'm surprised he didn't pull out a cow.

"Come on man. There's something out here." Ian says to his partner who was too engaged in my purse. Ian turns to me and aims the gun at me. I hear if go off and flinch, but it didn't seem to have been Ian's. The only thing I saw, was the other man flying towards the brick wall in front of us. A horrible crunching sound was heard when his body collided with the brick wall. He didn't get up or appear to be breathing. Ian turns around fast and starts shooting randomly in the direction his partner lay. He curses once he runs out of ammo. He calls out to his partner, while trading glances between his partner and whatever was in the dark that couldn't be seen.

"Brody! Get up man!" he yells. Brody didn't respond. Ian runs over to him and picks up his gun. I couldn't run. I was paralyzed as my back stayed against the cold brick wall. I saw a quick black blur pass in front of me. Whatever it was, it moved so fast that I felt the rush of wind hit me. Ian must've seen it too because he grabbed me and used me as a shield.

"Whatever game you're playing, you better stop! Or she dies! You hear me?! I will k-" he was cut off and before I knew what was happening, he was roughly yanked away from me. I couldn't see what was happening but it didn't take me long to guess, as I hear screaming and horrible gushing sounds followed by growling. His body was thrown into the side of the dumpster across from his partner. A pool of blood starts to pool around him. His stomach and throat were ripped out. Oh my god! No, no, no. This can't be happening! I couldn't believe what I was seeing. I waste no time in running for my life. When I get home, I make sure every window and every door was locked. I don't want whatever's out there to come here and fetch me. I was currently pacing back and forth in the kitchen while holding a metal baseball bat. I wasn't taking any chances. I jump as I hear a knock on the front door. I could feel sweat rolling down my back as my grip on the bat tightens. I slowly approach the door and carefully look through the peephole. I see the top of Adam's head. What was he doing here? I almost open the door but stop once I remembered what almost happened to me. How do I know that whatever's out there, doesn't have Adam knocking on my door? I hear a painful groan come from him and without thinking, I open the door. There he was, covered in blood. I drop the bat as an immediate response as to what I was taking in. His shirt was soaked in blood mainly over his chest and he looked as though he were about to lose consciousness.

"Annabelle." he weakly chokes out as he falls forward and into me. I almost fell too as I could barely handle his weight. I gently lay him on the floor and seal the entrance. He needs medical attention. I look over to the house phone that was on the wall right by the staircase. I began to advance to the house phone but was stopped when he grabs my arm. "No...no cops. You h-have to...get the bullets o-out." He says as he struggles to stay conscious. Was he serious?! He's on the floor dying and he doesn't want help?! I was about to get out of his grip and call for help but then I realized something too.
I couldn't talk...Oh my god, that meant no cops, no ambulance, no nothing. I could go get the neighbors, but what if that thing is out there waiting for me because I witnessed it kill those guys. Adam groans as his head moves slightly to the side. Panic begins to rise in me as realization dawns on me that I had a dream about him being shot...what if I could've prevented this by telling him? My breathing was uneven and it got really hot all of a sudden. I heard a high pitch ringing in my ears as everything moves in slow motion. I turn to look at Adam lying on the floor half conscious. I

could hear my heart beating in my ears as my breathing picked up. Adam's really here, bleeding out, and I don't know what to do. He groans again snapping me out of my panic session. Okay, okay.

"What do I do?" I mentally ask myself as I take deep breaths so I don't have an anxiety attack. I run into the kitchen and look for my dad's whiskey. I've seen this in a movie before. When someone got injured really bad, they'd pour alcohol on the wound to sterilize it. I search through three of the cabinets below before standing on the counter to reach the very top cabinets that only my tall dad could reach. Hopefully I don't fall and break my neck before I can save Adam. I open the first cabinet door relieved when I see that square bottle of Bourbon whiskey that my dad drunk on his "missing mom" days sitting abandoned in the corner. I didn't understand why he drank so much. I get the "missing mom part", but not even that could turn me to something like that. Once I firmly grip the bottle, I close the cabinet. I step down and my body freezes when I notice how quiet it is. The room was no longer filled with Adam's groans. Scared of what that might entail,

I race back to him to find his eyes were closed. He was very still, too still. I stand over him hoping to see his chest rise, indicating he was alive and breathing. When it didn't, I shake him a little as my breathing increased. He groans while holding his chest as his face frowns up in pain. Relief washes over me when I see him react. I don't know what I'd do if he died right here, right now. I gently move his hand from his chest and examine his torn, bloody shirt. How am I supposed to get the bullets out? I can't touch his wounds with my hands. Plus, the wounds were too small for me to even attempt to remove them. I need something small...Tweezers!
I run to my bathroom almost crashing into the sink because I was running so fast. I open my mirror and grab the blue tweezers sitting next to a bottle of "Tylenol". I approach Adam and use the small holes the bullets created, to tear open his shirt. I couldn't see through the blood so I pour whiskey on his wounds. Adam didn't budge at all. I couldn't believe what I was doing, let alone seeing. He had been shot in two places. One on the right and one on the left, right above his heart. I look up at him to see his eyes were still closed but his lips

were slightly parted. His chest rose ever so slightly while he wheezed every time he breathed out. I check for his pulse to find it was weak, almost not even present. I reach in with the tweezers and pull out the first bullet. It was smoking as if it were hot while a black liquid substance oozed out the top of it. I gag once the smell of rot hits my nose. It took all of my strength not to throw up. I pull out the second one and pour whiskey on both of his wounds. I get a cloth towel and dab his wounds gently. He needs help, I don't care what he says. He could die right here on my floor because of the amount of blood he's lost. I stand up and advance towards the front doors but stop once he speaks.

"Annabelle, please." he pleads, the pain sounding in his hoarse voice. I look at him and he looks at me with bloodshot eyes. His eyes weren't their normal brown color that I grew used to. They were a dark brown, almost black. "Stay. I need you here with me. Please." he begs as he looks into my eyes. Feeling that I should listen to him, it was in that moment that I couldn't refuse.

Chapter 8

The events from last night were still fresh in my mind as eyes flutter open. I see familiar pink walls as I sit up a bit disoriented as I look around. I was in my room. How was that possible when Adam was...unless that was a dream? Relief washes over me at the thought of last night not happening at all. I was thankful it was only a dream. I get up and look at my alarm clock. Next to it was a yellow sticky note.

"Thank you, Annabelle. You have no idea how grateful I am for you saving my life. Sorry for the whole putting you in bed type of deal. I just figured it would be weird if your parents came home and saw you sleeping on the floor." it read. At the bottom on the note Adam's name was written on it. As I let every word sink in, my shaking hands held the sticky note. It wasn't a dream after all...

*   *   *

I was currently sitting in chemistry, repeatedly tapping my pen against my purple notebook. The scene of Adam lying on the floor and me almost getting killed repeatedly plays in my mind like a broken record. I take a dep breath to calm myself from feeling overwhelmed. What if the people who shot Adam came looking for him here?! What if that's the reason why he's not here? All of the thoughts cycling through my head were too much for me. My chest starts to feel heavy.

"Annabelle, are you okay?" Mr. Wake asks me, but he sounded far away. I didn't know what was going on. It was like everything was in slow motion. "Annabelle?" Mr. Wake calls, but this time I could hear him loud and clear. I jump at the sound of his voice. The classroom fills with snickering people.

"The little freak didn't know we had a pop quiz today. Didn't know, that *that* of all things would shake her up." I hear Nina say which causes everyone to laugh.

"Enough!" Mr. Wake shouts. I feel my heart beating in my ears and with that I suddenly feel hot. "Hey," Mr. Wake says to me with concern written over his face. He was crouched down in front of my desk. One of his hand holding onto the front edge of my desk. Maybe if I go splash my face with cold water, I'll feel better. I stand up and as soon as I did, the room begins to spin. I stagger a bit almost losing my balance. I close my eyes and grip both sides of my desk. "Conner, go get the nurse." Mr. Wake orders as he stands up. He places a hand on my shoulder. Within minutes the nurse comes. I look up to see Tyler. What was the school's quarterback doing here? I look at him confused. Mr. Wake leaves my side as Tyler approaches me. He puts my arm over his neck while he put his arm around my waist. He guides me out of the classroom.

"I'm just gonna take you to the nurse office to lie down for a bit." he says as we continue down the hallway. The nurse office was a green room. On the walls were posters of what the inside of a human body looks like. There was also a poster advertising how important it is to get a flu-shot. He sits me down on a maroon bed that had a white paper sheet. I lay down and close my eyes. "You just sit tight while I prepare your vaccination." he says. Vaccination? My eyes pop open and I sit up. I look at him to see him already advancing towards me with an extra-long needle. Without warning, someone barges in. It was Ian, the guy who pulled me in the alley.

Startled by the interruption, Tyler turns to face Ian. Ian looks at me and smiles.

"You didn't think I actually died, did you? I told you I was going to take care of you, and I meant that." He says as he smiles wickedly at me.

"You can't be in here." Tyler says still holding the needle in his hand.

"Yeah..." Ian says as he takes a few steps towards us. His hand running along the top of the blue granite counter. "I thought you might say that." Ian says as he stops. One of his hands goes behind his back. He draws his gun and my breath gets caught in my throat as I'm filled with fear. I was once again paralyzed, unable to move. Ian doesn't hesitate as he points the gun at Tyler and pulls the trigger. I flinch at the loud noise the gun makes. Tyler's body falls backwards on the maroon computer chair. His head falls back as if he were looking up at the ceiling. His arms and legs were sprawled out. The needle hits the floor and I feel a few splashes of something warm hit my face. Out of instinct, I reach up and touch my face. When I pull my hand away, I see my fingers coated in blood. My breathing was shaky. I was going to die and I wanted to scream. I wanted to beg for my life, but I couldn't do anything as he points the gun at me. I jump awake from my nightmare at the sound of the bell. I look around disoriented to see students leaving the classroom. I had fallen asleep in class...I was never one to fall asleep in class. I glance up at the clock to see its 11:20am. It was already time for lunch. My eyebrows furrow together as I try to remember the events right before I dozed off. Then, just as on cue, memories of what happened floods my mind. When get to the class that Adam and I shared, his seat was empty. I watch the door hoping that he would walk in but he never did. I couldn't even focus on the lesson because my mind was everywhere but where it needed to be. I was too much into deep thought that I hadn't noticed I was sitting outside in my usual spot under the big oak tree that supported me with shade. I look up at the branch to see that same bird staring down at me. I couldn't bring myself to eat with everything buzzing around in my head. I pull out a book, thinking it would calm me down but soon as I read the first two words on the page, I feel the presence of someone standing nearby. I look up and there he was. Adam was standing there in a light grey shirt, white Vans, and black jeans. Before I could command myself to make a run for the door, he spoke.

"I know you have questions, but it's not safe to give you those answers. But I will tell you this, I was helping a friend who was in trouble. They needed me and if I hadn't showed up they wouldn't be here, alive." he says as he sits down next to me. As he did so, his eyes never left mine. I couldn't tell if he was crazed or what. The scene of Adam lying on that floor in the horrible state he was in and me being completely powerless to do anything about it, kept playing in my mind. With my notebook already out, I fish for a pen in my backpack.

"How are you still alive? You lost so much blood. I don't understand." I write to him. His mouth opens and closes before he says anything. It was like he was trying to come up with a lie.

"Uh, well I...i-it didn't hurt, that bad." Adam answers with uneasiness in his voice as he looks at me. He *was* lying to me.

"You should've died yesterday. There's no way anyone could have survived that." I write. Adam stays quiet a moment after reading it. This was scaring me. What if he was some sort of demon? I mean, it's not normal for someone to get shot one day and the next they're prancing around. All the thoughts running through my head of this situation soon became too much. I stand up abruptly, grab my things, and walk towards the door.

"Annabelle, wait!" Adam calls for me. Thankfully, he didn't follow me. I made sure to avoid him the rest of the day. I was going to need some time to process everything that happened. This wasn't something that happened everyday (at least not for me). When I get home, the aroma of beer smacks me in the face. I didn't have to guess who was home because sitting on the steps with an empty bottle of Bud Light beer in their hands was my dad. His eyes were red and he looked like he had been crying.

"Did you have a great day at school, sweetheart?" he slurs. Great, he's drunk. I nod my head and he stands up. He wobbles a bit before grabbing onto the wooden banister for support. "So, you didn't talk to any guys today, right?" he slurs. Before I could nod my head, he walks down the stairs and into the kitchen. I make my way upstairs quickly and quietly. I spend an hour doing nothing but thinking about Adam. I couldn't do homework without seeing his face. He's has to be some sort of demon. That didn't sound too crazy, right? There are so many things that are off setting about him. Last night's episode, the fight with Slade, and maybe I'm seeing things but his eyes change color. I know I can have a pretty wild imagination at times, but I know what I saw. I'm not crazy, come to think of it I'm not completely sane either. No-one is completely sane because normal is overrated. I'm yanked back to reality when I notice my dad yelling at me. I flinch as I realize how close he was as he stood in front of me. He crouches down in front of me and roughly grabs my face. He makes me look at him.

"What were you thinking about, Annabelle?" he slurs. His breath smelled heavy of alcohol. It takes everything in me not to rip his hands off my face and cover my nose. "Was it about a boy? Because I've been standing here talking for five minutes and you haven't acknowledged me!" he shouts in my face. Before I knew it, I was being pulled downstairs roughly by my hair and into the kitchen. I groan as he pushes me hard into the already cracked kitchen cabinet. I hear it break as I make contact with it. He moves fast to get something but I couldn't tell what it was because I was too busy dealing with the pain I had just encountered. Without warning, something was shoved down my throat. I didn't have a choice but to swallow it because I was kicked hard in the stomach. I panic as my taste buds adjust to the creamy but also drying texture known as "Peanut Butter". He was drunk and I was going to die if I didn't get my hands on my epi-pen soon. Before I could attempt to get up, he grabs my arm and drags me over to the sink. My throat slowly begins to feel small as it soon becomes difficult to breathe. His hand grips the back of my neck as he forcefully pushes my face into the sink. My heart pounds in my chest as fear courses through my body as I hear the facet running. He was going to drown me...I didn't want to die like this. I start to struggle, attempting to get out of his iron grip as I began gasping for air intently. "This is what happens when you're not focusing in school! This is what happens when you're too busy thinking about boys! If I'm not happy, you're not happy you little brat! Your mother left because of you!" he yells frantically. I feel myself fall backwards and hit the ground. I need my epi pen or else I wouldn't last longer. I try to roll over but stop as I'm greeted with a kick to my side. I open my mouth to scream but nothing comes out. I immediately curl myself into a ball as he continues to kick me. Each kick is harder than the last. Tears stream down my face as I feel my heart slowing down. My vision becomes blurry when as the desire to sleep takes over. My body relaxes on its own as my side grows with pain and numbness.

Chapter 9

I wake up on the floor in my room. I groan as I feel my entire body throb with an aching pain. Obviously, he wasn't too drunk *not* to kill me. I reach for my phone that was a few inches away from me and check for the time... It was 9:30am. I was an hour late. Crap! I force myself up only to groan as pain shoots through my body. After waiting for the pain to subside, I hop in the shower. I sigh in content as the hot water hits my newly bruised ribs, stomach, arms and my side. Now, I'm really going to have to wear long sleeves and it's not even winter! I'm going to look more like a freak because who wears long sleeves in the summer heat? It's about 98 degrees outside. When I finally convince myself that going to school is for the best, I start my walk to school. By the time I get there, I had one more class before lunch. Did I really take that long to get dressed? I walk into my history class and quietly go to my desk. I spot Adam out of the corner of my eye. Adam sits on the next row to my right and one seat behind me. I don't make eye contact with him, but I can feel his eyes on me. Mr. Hopkins was lecturing the class but he doesn't address me. As I approach my desk, I look down as I feel as though the class is watching my every move. Once I finally sit down, Mr. Hopkins addresses me.

"Nice of you to join us, Ms. Wood." he says with a slight nod. I give him a small smile as I feel my cheeks heating up a bit. He continues to lecture us and when he was done, he erases the chalk board. He then takes a seat in at his desk. The entire class is quiet. I watch him as he moves the papers around on his desk searching for something. He had to be about 5'2 and looked to be in his late thirties. He had a brown man bun, brown eyes, and a black beard. This never failed to throw me off. I mean, of course I've seen people dye their hair before. It was just, I've never seen a person with two different hair colors before.

"There you are." he says while picking up a piece of paper. He looks at it for a moment before he looks at me. "Now that you're here Ms. Wood, I can assign you a partner for the project that is going to be due at the end of next week." Project? I look over at Adam as I sense his intense staring. He looks in a different direction, almost as if not trying to get caught watching me. My eyebrows furrow together as I keep my eyes on him. "Mr....Vere." He says after a slight pause. I turn my attention to Mr. Hopkins. "You and Ms. Wood would make excellent partners. You both will be assigned to complete this project together. I will hand out the packet that will assign everyone to their assigned person to cover. If there are those of you who prefer instructions electronically, notify me by email no later than this Thursday." He says as he glances up at the clock. I look too and it says 10:29am.

"So close to lunch...almost there." I mentally tell myself.

"Well since we have some time left to kill, we'll start by getting ahead of schedule. We're going to explore one of my favorite chapters in this course," he pauses while smiling. "Now, this topic isn't going to be like the other chapters covered in this course. This is just a fun little chapter to get your minds going. We will be covering, "The Russian Sleep Experiment."" He says as his eyes widen with excitement. He opens his red and green book and tells us what page to turn to in ours. All throughout the lecture I could hear Adam trying to get my attention but I just ignore him. When the bell rings, I try to get my things as fast as possible so I can mix in with the crowd and lose him. That was interrupted when my history book fell on the left side of my desk. I lean over to retrieve it and instantly regret it as I feel my bruises stretch on my right side. I inhale a sharp breath and bite my tongue. Out of nowhere, I hear a low animalistic growl behind me that makes me sit up straight. That sound took me back to that night in the dark alley. I look around the classroom before my eyes lock on Adam who was shoving his belongings into his backpack. He wore an angry expression on his face and I'm willing to bet it's because I was ignoring him. I stand up and gather my belongings, ignoring the pain every time I move. I make it to my locker and my hand goes for the door when I start to feel a bit unbalanced. I let my warm forehead touch the cold locker. I close my eyes and take a deep breath.

  "Annabelle!" I hear a familiar Australian voice call out. Before I could open my eyes, I feel myself falling but something really warm catches me. I open my eyes to see that warm "something" was Slade. I look at him to see the concern look on his face. "Hey, are you okay?" He asks. I don't get a chance to respond because I'm greeted with darkness.

*   *   *

I was jumping on the trampoline with Adam in his backyard while our parents conversed amongst each-other inside the house. It was Adam's seventh birthday and all of his friends came over.

"Wanna play hide and seek?" Adam asks. I smile and say yes. We stop jumping and Adam stands on the edge of the trampoline. "Who wants to play hide and seek?!" Adam yells. Everyone starts jumping up and down with excitement. Adam and I get off of the trampoline.

"Since it's my birthday I get to be the seeker." Adam announces while smiling.

"Aww, but I want to be seeker." a girl says sounding disappointed.

"Shut up paisley! It's his birthday!" A girl with a few teeth missing says. Adam closes his eyes and starts counting, while everyone scatters into the house. It was just me and him outside. I didn't want to hide where everyone else did, so I look around observing the area.

"Four...Five...Six..." Adam counts. Maybe I could hide behind this tree, or in the dog shed. Adam knows I'm scared of dogs, but the dog was in the house. He wouldn't think to look there. As I approach the dog house, I notice someone watching me through the big gap in the brown wooden fence. The gap was big enough for someone my size to fit through. It was a boy with green eyes and jet-black hair. He motions for me to come over to approach him. "Fifteen...Sixteen..." Adam continues to count. I quickly tiptoe over to the boy and squeeze through the fence. "Okay! Ready or not! Here I come!" Adam shouts happily.

"He definitely would not find me here." I think to myself as a smile makes its way on my face.

"I'm Slade." The boy introduces himself to me.

"I'm Annabelle." I reply back.

"I came to say goodbye to Adam. I'm moving to Arkansas today." He says sounding sad.

"Oh. I'm sorry. Will you ever come back?" I ask.

"Well, my aunt lives here and she's getting married. I'll be at the wedding but...I don't think I'll move back." he says with the same sad tone in his voice.

"Well, maybe you can play with us until you have to leave. Come on." I says as I take his hand and lead him through the fence...

*　　　　　*　　　　　*

I wake up to Slade lightly shaking me.

"Annabelle?" he calls out. I blink a couple of times as it takes me a moment to realize what was going on. I just experienced a vivid flash back, which only meant one thing; I was stressing myself out more than I needed to. Concern was written all over his face.

"Y-you fainted...Are you okay?" He asks. I nod my head and attempt to get away from him, seeing how close we were. As a result of that, I end up feeling dizzy. I try to walk anyway and that only closes the distance between us as I soon find myself leaning into him. "Woah, woah. Easy now." He says as he helps me steady myself. I was so close to him that I could smell the cologne he wore. He looks at my lips and then back at me. That was a clear indication of what he wanted and he was *not* getting that from me. He clears his throat and looks me in the eyes this time. "Are you okay, for real this time?" he asks while chuckling at bit at the end. I nod my head once the dizziness goes away and put some distance between us. "Do you need me to walk you to lunch?" he offers. I decline his offer. "Well, if you need anything, I'm your guy." He says and with that he left me alone in the hallway. I watch him as he walks into a classroom. I wonder what went down between him and Adam. I would've never guessed that they were friends at any given point in time. The sad part, was Slade and I met before and I still had no clue as to who he was. I wonder if he remembered me? Maybe he did and just didn't say anything because he thought I wouldn't have remembered him (which he was right, up until now). After lunch, the rest of the day went by fast. Before I knew it, I was walking home. I couldn't shake the fear that coursed through me, as I thought about walking through the front door of my house. I was so sure my father was going to kill me. I didn't ask for this. I didn't ask for my mom to leave us; to leave me. Without her, I'm alone. I have no one to listen to me or to talk to. There's no one to hug me and tell me that things will get better even if it's a lie. I just want *someone* to be here for me. When I approach the porch, I hesitate before grabbing the house key on my lanyard. I open the door praying my dad wasn't on the steps like last time. I let out a breath of relief when I see the stairs free of my dad. I make a silent trip to my room. When I open the door, I stop abruptly as I see my dad in my room just standing there. He was thinking about something because he always messed with the stubble on his face. He had his back to me as he looks at the stuffed animals on my shelf.

"Alice." He says softly sounding like he was on the verge of tears. He sighs as he picks up the picture of my mom and I that was next to the stuffed Blue Stitch stuffed animal from *"Lilo and Stitch"*. I begged my mom to buy me him at Disney World six years ago. I missed her too, if not more. He wipes his eyes as he let out a quiet sob. This was quite the scene for me because I never saw my dad cry ever before. He took a deep breath as he wipes his face again. He turns around and his eyes snap to mine. He seems a little startled by this but quickly covers it up with an emotionless expression. "Well, I see *you're* home." he says, his voice hard again. I look down as he walks pass me. "Hurry up so I can eat. I have a big day tomorrow and I need to be in bed soon." he says sounding upset. I do my homework, cook dinner, and go off to bed on an empty stomach.

Chapter 10

The smell of bacon fills my senses as I walk down the stairs. I go to the kitchen and stop when I see my mom with her back turned to me. She was flipping pancakes.

"Alice! Where'd you put my watch at again?" I hear my dad yell.

"It's in the bathroom on the counter babe!" My mom yells as she turns around. Her eyes meet mine and I couldn't help the surprise look that took upon my face.

"Mom?" I hear the words come out of my mouth as tears fill my eyes.

"Annabelle sweetie, what's wrong?" she asks with concern written all over her face. Without hesitation, I run to her and embrace her in a hug.

"Hey." She says softly as her warm arms wrap around me. I close my eyes savoring the moment until she pulls back to look at me. When she opens her mouth to speak, she was cut off by my dad.

"Guess who just got a promotion." he says while fixing his blue and grey checkered tie. He was dressed in a white-collar shirt with black dress pants. No one responded. "This guy!" he says while pointing to himself. He approaches a plate of bacon that was on the counter. I was amazed at what I was seeing. His face was free of facial hair and his hair was nicely combed back. He no longer looked like his tired self.

"Will, that's great." my mom says. She approaches him and fixes his tie. I wipe my face and watch them interact.

"You were always terrible when it came to ties." My mom says with a smile.

"Well, good thing I have a beautiful wife like you by my side." he says as he gives her a peck on the lips.

"Oh, I almost forgot," my mom says as she turns to me. "Adam's out-front waiting for you. He said something about a carnival?" My mom says sounding unsure. I feel my face contort in confusion. Adam? What is he doing here?

"Well if that's the case, I want you home by 10 o'clock, little lady. I know how guys are these days." I hear my dad say to me.

"Will, Annabelle's a smart girl like her mother. She knows the do's and don'ts..." I hear my mom say. The conversation between my parents fade as I approach the door. I open the door only to be greeted by a dark alley. It was the alley I got pulled in and was almost killed. I heard that same animalistic growl I heard in class. I scream as I feel myself being sucked in by an unknown force. I awake from slumber with a gasp up. My back was left damp as I try to catch my breath. I don't know how much more of these dreams I can take. I almost jump out of my skin when my alarm unexpectedly goes off. I look over and it was 7:20am. I could have slept in an extra minute (don't judge, every minute counts). I sigh and fall back onto my pillow as I close my eyes ignoring the alarm.

"Annabelle! You up yet?!" I hear my dad yell from beneath me. It's not like I could reply. I did the only thing that was close to a response; I hit the wall with the side of my fist two times. "Alright, get moving then." I hear my dad respond below me. I take the shortest shower ever and I make my down stairs to retrieve the lunch I made the previous night before. I then wait in my usual spot in the living room. I sit on the white couch we've had since my parents moved in together after 3 years of dating in the late 80's. It still looks as if it were brand new. My mind goes back to that night when Adam came knocking on my door. I know what he said, but I just can't wrap my mind around what happened. I saw flashes of Ian's face as he aimed the gun at me. I could still hear the gunshots and the growls followed by each horrible gushing sound.

"Come on. Let's go." My dad says which earns a slight jump from me. He went to approach the door and paused. He looks back at me as I stand trying to look like I normally did in the mornings, because my face always told what I was feeling. "What's the matter with you?" He asks in a harsh tone. I shake my head. "I'm not going to ask you again." He says while giving me a look. I point to my head. "Headache huh? Your little headache is nothing compared to the headache you give me every day. Now let's go, I'm running late today thanks to you." He says as he walks out the door. The ride to school was spent with me thinking of how things could have gone. What would have happened if that thing hadn't showed up? Adam would have died if I had gotten killed.

"Get out." My dad says interrupting my thoughts. I didn't notice we were here all ready. I got out of the truck and made my way to the doors.

"Annabelle!" I hear Adam's voice behind me. I stop as I feel my body tense. My eyes go wide. Oh god, please let my dad be gone. Please don't let him see us. I look over to where my dad's black truck was just parked, only to find him turning onto the main road. I breath out relived at this sight. "Hey." Adam says as he playfully bumps into me. I smile at him and we walk inside together. My first class went by pretty fast but once I got to geometry, it was non-stopped harassment day for Slade. He just wouldn't leave me alone. I mentally roll my eyes as he opens his mouth to speak.

"So, tell me," he says as he conjures up a smirk on his face. "Are you, busy by any chance today. There's this concert that starts at—" I cut him off by waving my hand in protest. I was not a party person and if I was, I wouldn't go partying with him. "Let me guess, not a party person." He says. I shake my head and return back to my classwork. He's quiet for a moment before he speaks again. "Look, I know I'm seen as the "bad guy" around here, but you got it all wrong. Adam...he made me this way." I look at him. His face was serious this time. He chuckles a bit. "We weren't always this way towards each-other. The hate, I mean. There was a time where we were really close. So close, you could have called us brothers..." he trails off. He opens his mouth to speak again but was cut off by Ms. Nicks.

"Back to work, Mr. Tyler." Ms. Nicks says, as she looks at Slade from behind her desk. She held a magazine in her hands. I mentally scoff at her. We both follow her instructions, but I couldn't help but wonder what happened between those two. I wanted to ask if he ever remembered me being in the picture but something told me now wasn't the time. When the bell for lunch sounds, he takes off in a rush before I can get his attention. So much for having a conversation. I go to my locker to retrieve the same lunch I make every night before school, when I sense a presence behind me. I turn around expecting it to be Adam, but it was Margie.

"Listen up, *mute,* Adam and I have known each-other for a very long time." She states while folding her arms. There were a few moments of silence before my eyes move side to side and then at her. "Which means, that we have quite the history. Which also means, he's off limits. Especially to someone like *you*. I mean, come on mute, do you honestly believe that he'd ever consider—" I cut her off by me walking away from her. I don't have time for this "*Mean Girls*" crap.

"Did she just..." I hear her trail off, asking herself as I walk away. A warm hand was suddenly laces with mine. I turn to see it was Adam.

"Hey" he says as he smiles at me. I look down at our hands and back at him as I feel butterflies in the pit of my stomach. "Don't pull away. I know Margie is giving you a hard time, so if she thinks we're dating maybe she'll back off and stop with her death threats." He says as we continue to walk.

"What is *happening* in this place!" I hear Margie yell in frustration. I smile a bit knowing that this got to her. Serves her right for all the trouble she's caused me all. Adam and I walk to my usual spot under the tree. He gently let's go of my hand and I instantly feel cold without the warmth his hand provided. I look at the grass as it wobbles a bit from the warm breeze.

"I know you're still upset about what's going on and you have every right to be." Adam says as he fiddles with his thumbs. I look at him and to see his eyebrows slightly furrow. I'm grateful for the save with Margie, but this doesn't change how I feel with everything that's happened. He then looks up at me, his face serious.

"Yesterday, in class, I saw some bruises on you and I can't help but think—" I interrupt him by waving my hands and grabbing a piece of paper.

"I was racing my cousin Duke at the soccer field in "Blooms", and me being me I tripped over my own two feet and I went tumbling down the hill." I write down. My heart was racing. I had never thought of a lie so fast in my life. He reads it and then looks at me.

"Are you sure? I mean, are your parents... is there someone hurting you?" he asks with concern. I shake my head and smile to reassure him.

"I know it's been a while since we've seen each-other but don't tell me you've already forgotten how clumsy I am." I write in a joking manner. He chuckles, but it wasn't genuine. It was almost as if he didn't believe me.

"Yeah, you were always the clumsy one." He says. To make it seem more real, I playfully push him while smiling and shaking my head. He chuckles again. Adam pulls out a packet from his back pack and hands it to me. I look at him. "It's our assignment for history. I wanted to get a head start in the class and I figured you would too, so I may or may not have snagged it from the teacher's desk." He says as he rubs the back of his neck. I shake my head at him and he lets out a small chuckle. I open the packet and at the top in bold it reads: "You all will be putting together a slide show for the class, that will talk about your person from the 70's. You will tell what this person did, followed by pictures, and a few fun facts." I look below the instructions and to see a list of names followed by the assigned person for that group. I see our last names and next to it was "Leslie Uggams". I knew her, she was an African American singer and actress in the 70's. I remember we did a report on her for black history month and someone in my class go to present her to the class.

"I've never heard of her before, but that's what school's for." Adam says as he stands up. I look at him a bit confused. "I'm coming back. Bathroom." He says while leaving his back pack on the ground next to me. I continue flipping through the packet to see what everyone else had. I saw someone had Frederick Douglass, Sigourney Weaver,

Richard Nixon, The Beatles and other people. I sit the packet down and look over at Adam's backpack. It was slightly unzipped. I can't help the sudden temptation I feel. All of my answers could be sitting right next to me, or at least some. He was lying to me and I wanted answers. After about a minute of contemplating, I reach over and grab his backpack. I open it to only find two notebooks and a folder. There was a mini blue composition book and I pick it up. Adam had just left, so I only had a few minutes to look and put everything back to the way that it was. I open the book and see drawings of things I've never seen before. They looked like they were ancient sketches. There was one I liked in particular. It was a sketching of a wolf, standing on a cliff at night over-looking a forest. I continue to flip through some more pages until I come across a sketch of a woman. She was leaning on a balcony, looking up at the sky. She looked vaguely familiar. I wasn't sure where I'd seen her before. I continue to stare at the woman trying to figure out why she looked so familiar to me. It's not like I go out and explore the world.

"You know, going through someone's stuff while they're gone might say that you don't trust them or that you're not to be trusted." I slightly jump as I hear Adam speak. I look over at him to see him leaning on the tree beside me. He doesn't even look upset that I was going through his things. He simply sits next to me and gently takes the book from me. "I carry this around with me everywhere I go." He says while looking at the book. I look at him to see his facial expression is serious. "I got into art a long time ago but then something, personal happened and I haven't gotten the chance to get back to it." he explains. I went to grab paper to apologize but was stopped once he gently put his hand on top of my mine. "You don't have to apologize. I mean, I guess it's expected with everything that's happened." He pauses, his eye still on the book. "Annabelle, I want you to know that what I told you is the truth, okay?" He said as he looks into my eyes. "You're my best friend and I know that given everything you've gone through, won't change how you feel. I just want you to know you can trust me." He says. I now found myself conflicted. Part of me wants to trust him and part of me is screaming danger. There were too many questions that couldn't be answered.

"We have a project to do and after that project's over, I think we need to put some space between us. It's not permanent. It's just so I can take time to process everything." I write to him.

"Yeah, okay." He says once he reads the paper. He opens his mouth to speak but was cut off by the bell. "Well, I guess I'll see you later then." He says as we both stand after gathering our things. We go our separate ways and once school was over, I end up hiding in the bathroom.

I did *not* want to bump into Adam or Slade today. I only want to see them when I absolutely have to. After waiting several minutes, I peek out the door to see an empty and quiet hallway. I sigh in content as I step out and proceed to my normal route. Once I get home, I waste no time in opening my backpack to get my notebook. That moment was short lived when I notice Adam's mini blue composition notebook resting on top of my red math book. He must've slipped it in when I wasn't looking. I smile a bit as I open the book to see my favorite drawing. I then go back to the drawing that I couldn't put my finger on.

Without warning my door was opened and I was greeted with my father.

"Annabelle, I won't be home tomorrow so you can eat and all that stuff." He says while looking at me. I nod having been a little startled. His eyes look around my room before he shut the door reluctantly. I let out a breath of relief as I look at the drawing once more before putting it in my backpack so I could focus on my homework.

Chapter 11

"You came." I hear that same feminine familiar voice. The tone was a mixture of happiness and surprise. All of a sudden, I was standing in front of the same crowd of people. I recognized this place. This is where I was at in my dream. I was hugging someone (or should I say Tabitha). I scan the crowd searching for my mom (at least I could move my eyes). She was nowhere to be seen. The person pulls back for me to see it was that same Asian woman that approached Tabitha. She was the lady from Adam's drawing.

"My dearest sister. I wouldn't miss this for the world." The woman says as she pulls back and flashes a sad smile.

"Nick is in trouble. You have to help him. You have to find him. It can't be them. You have to be the one to lead her to him. If you don't, they'll all die. They will find him and when they do—" Tabitha whispers but is cut off by Hansel telling them it was time to call it a wrap. The woman steps back with a sad expression as she takes one look final look at me (or I guess I should say Tabitha). Her eyes held promise as she gave a slight nod before returning to the crowd. Hansel reaches in his blazer and pulls out a knife. He advances towards me after two men from the crowd grabs both of my arms and hold me still. No, I didn't want to see this. A loud noise that was not recognizable, pierces the sky. It was so loud that everyone had to cover their ears. The ground starts to shake and people began to fall because of the violent shaking the loud noise brought. The knife falls on the ground as I stagger and eventually find the ground. Was this an earthquake? I find my way to the knife and grab it. I manage to stand up through the violent shaking of the earth.

"No! You will not escape your fate! You've caused enough trouble Tabitha!" I hear Hansel yell and before I can turn to look at him, he tackles me to the floor. The knife flies out of my hand.

"You knew how this would end." Tabitha spits with venom. I watch through her eyes as she wrestles and grapples with Hansel until he is on top of her. He puts his hands around her neck in attempt to strangle her. I can feel the tightness of his grip on my neck. I wasn't even Tabitha but yet I could feel it as if I were her. Tabitha claws at his arms while gasping for air.

"My dearest daughter, you brought this upon yourself." He says as a pained expression washes over his face. Behind him the sky is now grey and cloudy. I see a few leaves blowing in the whipping wind. My vision becomes blurry as Tabitha struggles to breath.

"Please." She barely manages to get out. Everything slowly dims until all I can see is darkness. I jump awake from slumber but this time, I awaken with a panic attack. I'm panting and gasping for air like I've ran a marathon. I put my head between my legs like the doctors told me to. I try to take deep breaths to calm down. After a few minutes, I start to feel like myself. Something in the corner of my eye catches my attention. I turn my head to see it was Adam's sketch book. The book was opened and the drawing of the Asian lady stared at me. I quickly close the book. That has to be why she looked so familiar, but why did Adam have a drawing of her? Was she a real person or was she appearing in the artist's dream too? I prop my pillow up against the headboard before laying back on it. I stay like that pondering and trying to conjure up a reasonable answer that explained everything. It takes a few minutes when I realize the only way to get answers was to ask the man himself. I make my way downstairs after cleaning up. I still loved how quiet the house was without my dad's presence. I advance to the refrigerator to fetch my lunch, when I see a sticky on the fridge.

"Breakfast is in the microwave and money for lunch is on the table in the hallway by the front door." It read. After reading it, I had to read it again because I was shocked that he'd give me money AND fixed breakfast for me. I didn't even know he *could* cook. The only times he cooked were for mom's birthday, and the menu always stayed the same. I go to the microwave and see that there were two pancakes with bacon and eggs. My stomach growls at the sight. I warm the plate up and take it to the table. It actually looked and smelled good. I was a bit hesitant to take the first bite, but after I convinced myself that there was nothing worse than being poisoned, I scarf the whole meal down. I glance at the time on the stove and decided that I couldn't delay the inevitable any longer. I only make it to the stop sign down the street from my house before Adam shows up in his "bat mobile". This cannot be a habit of his. He gets out of the car with a smile on his face as he speaks to me.

"Man, it sure is hot today. It would be such a shame if you had to walk *all* the way to school with only ten minutes to spare." He says in a teasing manner as he opens the passenger door for me. I roll my eyes as I smile. I wanted to refuse his offer but my body disobeyed me. Once he got in he looks over at me. "You smell like syrup," He says before he puts the car in drive. Out of instinct I smell my shirt, which earns a chuckle from Adam. I feel my face heat up a bit as I realize what I just did. God, why am I so weird? "Don't worry. I'm sure all the boys like the smell of syrup." He says as he breaks out into laughter. I playfully hit him in the shoulder which causes him to laugh even more. When we approach a red light, I look over at him. I give him a serious face which causes him to sober up. "Hey, I'll still like you. No matter what." He says while snickering. I shake my head and look out the window as we take off. When we get to our destination, he opens the door for me and I get out. "Margie alert." Adam says to me as he shuts the door. I look amongst the people who were all crowding in front of the door. They appear to be waiting for the doors to open, which is weird because that never happens. I see a boy leaning against the brick wall listening to music and a few other people imitating him. I continue to scan the crowd looking for Margie. Dressed in a bright highlight green Nike hoodie, was Margie. She was talking to a guy who didn't seem so interested in what she had to say. I'm pulled from my thoughts when I feel Adam's warm hand lace with mine. Butterflies erupt in my stomach and I knew that with everything that was going on, this was the last thing I should be feeling. He looks at me and smiles. I smile back, as I'm left with an emotion I can't describe. We approach the crowds of people.

"Wonder what's the hold up." Adam says as he stands on his tippy toes, trying to see over the crowd. It would be nice if school were cancelled. That way I could study and start on our project.

"Well, if school *is* cancelled I guess we could—" Adam was cut off by a very familiar Australian accent.

"Well would you look at that. I guess this means I get to skip school after all." We turn around to see Slade. His eyes traveled down at our hands, as the smirk fades off his face. "Well, if it isn't Hollywood's finest couple eh?" He says as he looks at Adam and then at me. I see his jaw tightens as his face is filled with anger. Was this making him...jealous? Oh my gosh, I cannot be *that* person. I just can't be. Without warning, I unlace our hands and Adam looks at me surprised. Slade chuckles. "Well looks like I'm not the only one on the "I hate Adam committee." Slade says as a smirk reappeared on his face. He looks at me before glancing at Adam. Before I could hear what Adam was going to say, I squeeze through the crowd and made my way up to the front.

"Annabelle!" I hear Adam's voice. I just need to get pass this project and then I can steer clear of him for the rest of this year. Eventually the doors open and we all flood in. Class starts like the usual and when lunch happens, I end up going to the cafeteria to buy myself a lunch. I've only ever been in the lunchroom twice and that was my freshman and my sophomore year.

"Maybe it's as many people in there as there were." I mentally say trying to work up my confidence. Something told me otherwise. I sigh as I open blue double doors. I'm hit with many voices and the aroma of food. There were three floors with lunch tables. The highest floor had mostly sport teams and the second and first floor were just other students. I look around for the lines to see what food was available. On the red wall and white wall, there were three neon that said "American", "Tex-Mex", and "Subs". Not caring what I ate, I got in the shortest line, which happened to be the sub line. The lines on both sides of me were terribly long and yet there were only about seven people in front of me. I guess they are really determined to get whatever they want.

"Hey." I hear Slade say behind me. I turn around to see him standing with both hands in his jean pockets. I wave with a light smile and he chuckles. I look at him confused as to what's funny. He sobers up. "So, how's your day been going?" He asks. Great, until you showed up to harass me. I put a thumb up and he nods his head. "That's good." He says and after that he didn't say anything else until after we both bought our lunches. I advance to the door that had my favorite spot waiting for me on the other side. Slade was right behind me. I tense a bit and stop at the door. Please don't let Adam be there waiting for me. I then turn and face Slade which results in him looking at me. "What? I can't see you safely to your spot?" He asks. I shake my head. "Fine, have it your way." He says as he walks in front of me and out the door.

I hold my breath thinking I would hear yelling but it was quiet. I open the door to see only Slade sitting down taking a bite out of his sub. I'm betting I might have upset Adam. I'd rather have that than Slade come out here to see Adam waiting on me. I sigh in relief as I approach my spot. Can't these two leave me be? I'm trying to get a grasp on everything that's happened. It's hard to do that when I feel like I'm a toy that's being fought over. I guess it serves somewhat of a distraction but distractions can only last so long. I shake my head as I get a few images of the Asian lady. I shake my head and take a deep breath to calm my mind before I grab my book. After minutes of munching and reading, he speaks.

"So, are you really on the "I hate Adam Committee?" He asks. I shake my head.

"Hate is a strong word, but I don't particularly dislike him either." I write to him. He scoffs once he reads the paper.

"I don't see what you see in him. If anything, he's not good for you. He'll get you to care about him but in the end, he'll never be able to protect you." He says getting upset.

"I don't need protection. I can take care of myself." I write to him.

"Oh yeah?" And how has that worked out for you!" He practically yells at me. I look into his eyes to see a darker shade of green. I blink a bit as my eyebrows furrow as I go to get a better look but he stands up abruptly. "I'm sorry. I shouldn't have...I gotta go." He says looking a bit strained. He quickly makes his way back inside the building. I'm left stuck in place as I take in what happened. What did he mean by "how has that worked out for me?" I go through memory lane as I try to think of anything that happened to me. Other than that night when...Was he talking about that night I almost got murdered? How could he have... I'm sure he meant something else by it. I push my tray away from me as I suddenly wasn't hungry anymore. I mean what else could he have meant by that? He wasn't there, but how could he have known that? Unless...no. No, I need to stop thinking about this. It doesn't make sense and only a crazy person would think like that. He meant something else...yeah. The bell rings, which makes me jump. I clean my area and retreat back to class. Sadly, I can't think because one, Adam wasn't in class and two I was too distracted by what happened with Slade. Could that be a connection? After school, I take my normal route on foot to get home. When I arrive, I take a long shower to help clear my thoughts, which doesn't help. Why wasn't Adam in class. He gave me a ride to school this morning. Was it because I let go of his hand? I'm currently lying in bed staring at my ceiling as my mind continues to throw thoughts at me. I really need to stop because I'm only going to give myself a headache. I open the door to my terrace and walk outside. I look up to see the crescent moon sticking out like a sore thumb in the dark sky. That was the best part about it being night time; the stars and the moon. I'm not sure how long I stayed out on the terrace just watching the sky.

Chapter 12

I groan as I sit up. I've been tossing and turning all night. Judging by the lighting in my room, I knew I'd have to get up soon. I might as well up now and get an early start on my routine. At least I'll get to spend a minute more in the shower. I enter my room from the bathroom once I'm dressed and put my backpack on. I head downstairs in the kitchen to retrieve my lunch. Before I could grab my lunch out of the refrigerator, the doorbell rings. Were we expecting guests? We never have people over. The door to our backyard opens without warning and as a result I jump.

"That might be my friend coming to help with—" my dad says but stops and I watch his facial expression change as he breaks out into laughter. I stay frozen as I move my eyes side to side. I didn't see what was so funny. "Oh man, oh...That is the most you have made me laugh." He says while wiping a tear off his face.

"And that's the first time in a long time since I've heard *you* laugh." I thought back.

"Now, grab me a beer if you will and get one for my friend and point him this way." he orders as he closes the door. The doorbell rings again. "Don't keep him waiting! We need to be on the road in less than an hour!" I hear my father yell from the other side of the door. I grab my lunch before opening the front door.

"I'm not exactly sure what I did wrong but I hear flowers make the perfect forgiveness request. Will flowers make up for what happened yesterday?" Adam asks as he stands on my porch holding flowers in on hand while the other was in his pocket. He smiles hopefully at me. I quickly glance behind me as I push him with one hand outside making sure to close the door behind me with the other hand. I give him the "What are you doing here?" look. "I'm gonna take that as a no?" he says it as a question, giving me a confused look. I point to his car. "So, you do like the rides I offer?" he asks as a smirk forms on his face. Not wanting to waste another second, I grab his arm and lead him towards his car. "Eager, are we?" he asks as he hands me the flowers. He opens the door for me and he get in on the driver's side. He takes off and I couldn't be any happier. When we approach the stop sign at the end of my street, I let out a shaky breath. That would not have ended well if my dad decided to answer the door. That was too close for my liking. Adam looks over at me. "Are you okay?" he asks. I look at the roses and smile.

"Thank you." I mouth to him.

"Yeah, don't mention it. But you didn't answer my question. Are you sure you're okay?" He presses. I nod my head and smell the flowers. I could tell he didn't believe me but I was thankful he let it go. When we arrive at our destination, Adam turns the car off and I get out instead of waiting on him to open the door for me. I make my way to the building and Adam catches up to me. "Talk to me." He says while swinging his backpack around his shoulder. I continue to walk, not bothering to glance his way.

"Annabelle?" He says. I look over at him and put a finger to my lips indicating for him to be quiet. He looks at me in confusion but he does as I say. We continue to walk silently inside the building and when it was time, we part ways. I'm currently in geometry tuning out Ms. Nicks. I couldn't focus with my mind wondering what would have happened if my dad saw Adam on our doorstep. He probably wouldn't remember Adam because it's been so long. I mean, I didn't even *recognize* him at first so surely my dad would only jump to the conclusion of Adam being my boyfriend (and bringing me flowers would only confirm his conclusion). Which would not end well for me.

"And there she is." I hear a familiar Australian accent say. I look to where the voice spoke and it was Slade. I give him my best convincing smile.

"You think you can fool the trick master at hand?" He says. I give him a confused look. "I can tell somethings bothering you." He says. I shake my head and gave him a smile. "Look, I'm not saying you should talk about it to me but talking about things help. I would know the most about that. I lost someone very special to me and I blamed my brother for it. I never forgave him even though at the end of the day, family sticks together and well, I didn't stick with him... and I'll never stick with him." Slade says as tears form in his eyes while a hateful expression takes over his face. "And I don't regret it." He adds, his voice hard as his jaw flexes. I didn't know what to say. What could I say? "Right," Slade clears his throat. "Enough of my story." He says as he blinks a couple of times, trying to sound nonchalant.

"Alright, I'm going to read off a list of names and if your name is called, then you are failing this class. Extra credit to boost your grade will be offered but you must do your work in here during our 30-minute lunch break." Ms. Nicks says catching both of our attention. I then zone out as she starts reading the names which I was certain my name would *never* be on that list. When lunch comes around Adam was waiting for me at the door.

"It's not too late to turn around Annabelle." I mentally tell myself. "It's not too late." He smiles lightly when he sees me.

"Can you tell me what's wrong?" He asks as he holds open the door for me. We walk over to the shaded area and sat down under the grey stormy clouds. I don't look at him but I can feel his eyes watching me as I went in my backpack to get a pencil and paper. I didn't want to tell him that if my dad sees him I'll get the worst beating of my life. Or better yet, I'm not allowed to befriend anyone because my dad fears that I'll seek aid from someone. I tell him the only thing I can. I tell him that he can never show up to my house unannounced like that ever again. He agrees and continues to watch me, as if he were looking for something.

"I get it." He says after I take a bite of my sandwich. I look over at him. "You don't have to tell me. Just know if you want to talk about it, I'm here and I will listen. Always." He says while looking at me. I nod my head and give him a smile. He smiles in return. "Is there a way we can work on that project today by chance?" He asks.

Today was close enough with Adam almost getting seen on my porch. I shook my head. I need to figure out what days my dad will be home.

"My dad and I have some family that will be staying with us so I'm not sure what my schedule will look like." I write to him. This I knew I could get away with because when Adam and I were younger, my aunt and my cousin would come here to visit us right around this time. They always came three weeks before our spring break. "Oh, that's right. This is around the time they come here for visits." Adam says. I nod my head and smile.

"How's Brendon? Is he still working on punts?" He asks. Brendon is my cousin and he's only a year younger than me. Even though Adam and I were close, Brendon and Adam were close as well. They were either playing football or wrestling. Brendon plays football for his church as well as track. I remember he would have the hardest time doing punts and kicking the ball in the goal. Adam never failed to help him practice after school. I smile as I remember those times which earns a chuckle from Adam. I shake my head.

"Good, because if he doesn't have it now, he won't have it." Adam says. I shake my head at him. He chuckles once more. "Tell him I said don't be a stranger." He says. I make a donut hole with my index finger and thumb as if to say "Okie dokie." We eat the rest of our lunch and luckily this time I was able to eat all of my mine. I was the last one to leave my last class all because my English teacher wanted to tell me how great my persuasive essay was. When she was done, she wished me well for the rest of the week all while giving me pointers on how to better my writing. I make my way to my locker and once I gather my belongings, I head towards the exit. My blood runs cold as I see my dad sitting on the red bench in the hallway next to the doors. Why was he waiting inside? He never waited inside. I mentally tell myself to calm down as I approach him. He had his head turned towards the glass doors as he watched the rain. When he noticed my presence, he stands up abruptly as his eyebrows frowned.

"Let's go." He says.

He reaches on the side of the bench and grabs a black umbrella I didn't acknowledged was there. He hands it to me and advances to the door. I was a bit taken back from this. We walk in silence to his car in the rain as he walks on the side of me without anything to shield himself. When we get in the car, no words were said expect him asking if my day at school was good. It was the same thing once we got home. I was confused because I expected him to say something as to why I just took off without saying goodbye. Or maybe why I didn't bring him his beer, but he didn't utter a single word to me.

I'm currently in my room doing my homework when my dad barges in.

"One of the neighbors were killed and I'm going over there to check it out. Don't come out this house unless told otherwise." He instructs and I nod my head. A neighbor was killed? I was instantly taken back to that night I was almost killed. The night Adam came to me and I almost couldn't do anything to help him.

That night I felt helpless. What if whatever killed Ian and Brody came here looking for me and decided to pick a different target? I feel my heart rate pick up along with my breathing. Someone could've died because of me. Everything starts to spin as it suddenly got really hot in my room. I gently laid down on my bed and sigh as the cold pillow touches my face. I take two deep breaths and mentally tell myself that it's okay.

Chapter 13

I hiss in pain as the razor nicks the skin on my left leg. I put the razor down as I see a little streak of blood run down my leg. I'm sitting on the edge of the tub wrapped in a towel. This is exactly why I don't make much effort to shave my legs. They weren't that bad (just don't let the light from the sun hit them). Who would see them anyway? I continue to shave and once I finish, I make my way to my parent's room. The smell of beer hits me and I notice my dad left the door slightly open. I push open the door to see the window open and his bed made. This room looked completely different than the last time I was in here. Mom's dresser was no longer in its' normal spot under the window. The pictures of her and dad were no longer hanging on the walls. The only thing that was left behind were the shapes that outlined the portraits. I'm not saying I completely hate the giant light squares and rectangles on the light blue walls, I just never thought he'd actually take them down. I look around the room with only my eyes and see that the main big dresser they shared still had her jewelry and perfume on it. I advance to the dresser and pick up her favorite perfume in that red glass bottle.

I take a whiff of it and I smile. I can't help the tears that form in my eyes. He kept everything of hers. It was almost like she never left. I used to come in here all the time just to smell her shirts and sweaters; sometimes her perfume. I couldn't describe the feeling I always got when I came in here. It was like she was here with me. Maybe I feel the way I do because I so desperately want her to hold me. I wouldn't even care why she left, just as long as she promised never to leave again. I miss her so much. I often wonder why she didn't take me. She could have waited for dad to fall asleep and together we could have snuck out in the night and never looked back. We could be doing mother-daughter things right now. We could be at a beach or getting our nails done. It's sad to say and to accept that some things are the way that they are. I silently sob as I find it hard for me to fight for control. I can't go on like this. I have to stop thinking about her. I have to stop thinking about this room, stop coming here, and I have to try to move on. I see her black sweater draped over the computer chair that she always sat on. She called it "Mommy's' workspace." I smile as tears run down my face as I remember her telling me how I gave it that name. I was only two years old and I could hardly speak but I knew what "Mommy's workspace" was. I hear the trees ruffle against the wind and that brings my attention to the open window. I go over to close it and was stopped when I heard a beer bottle gently bump against another one. I quickly turn around to see my dad standing in the doorway. My heart beats faster and the sudden sadness I once felt was replaced with fear.

"What are you doing in here?" He asks with that voice I'm used to right before he gets in his mood. I stand still and look at the floor. Once again, the ruffling of the tress against the wind sounds again. "Well aren't you going to close it?" he asks as he takes a sip of his beer that I didn't notice he had. I look at him once more and swallow.

"Get out." He says in a stern voice that made my feet move on its own accord. Before I could get pass him, he grabs my arm roughly and this time I didn't even flinch. "If I ever catch you—" he stops short and looks at me. I watch his eyes move, as they analyze my face. His frown disappears and he gently let's go of my arm. "I guess I should get you to school. You don't need to be late." He says in a different tone I wasn't used to. It almost sounded...nice. To say I was taken back by this was an understatement. He takes one last sip of his beer and walks out the room leaving me stuck in place. The ride to school was quiet except for the radio that was broadcasting about the neighbor who died last night. My dad turns down the volume on the radio.

"There's some crazy guy on the streets stabbing people for money. I don't want you outside this house unless you're going to school or coming home from school, especially since I won't be home for a couple of days. I'm leaving today and I've set out more than enough money for you to order in." He says as he parks the car in a parking space instead of driving up to the side walk and letting me out. I was getting scared at his sudden actions. He never parked the car. I look over at him as he did with me.

"I know you miss your mother. I miss her too Bee." He says using the nickname he came up for me. He dug in his brown leather jacket pocket and pulled out an envelope that had so many creases from being folded a number of times. He hands it to me. It looked like it had been through a lot along with a few stale brown stains on it.

"She left it on the kitchen counter along with the note to me. She said she wanted you to have it." He says while looking at me. I didn't know how I felt about all this. I mean sure I missed my mom. I miss her everyday but this...I didn't know what to think. I look at my dad to see his eyes barely watering. I could tell he was trying to not to cry.

"Now," he says, his voice hard as he put the truck in reverse. He drives up to the side walk and unlocks the door. "Go before you're late to class." He says while looking away. I look at him as I didn't know what was happening. Why was he being so...nice to me? Why give me that letter now when you've had it all this time. Why not keep it for yourself? He turns back to me as his eyes were filled with more tears.

"Now!" He yells causing me to flinch and go for the door. He drives off the second the door shuts. I stare down at the envelope in my hand. I couldn't breathe and I didn't want to. I didn't know what to expect from this letter. However, I did know one thing; this could be what I longed for. This could explain the reason why she left. Even though my dad told me she left because of me, I want to hear it from her. I need to know if what my dad said is true.

"Well if it isn't the beauty herself." I hear a familiar voice say. I jump as I hear the voice directly behind me. I turn to see who this familiar voice belonged to and it was Slade. "Feeling better, today are we?" He asks. I slightly smile and nod my head. He had his hands shoved in his black jean pockets. He smirks a bit like he always did whenever I was looking at him.

"Shall we?" he says as he sticks out his hand as if to say "after you". "I hope you don't mind me walking you to your class today. Believe it or not, I need to speak with Mr. Wake." He explains.

I nod my head. I guess I could use a brief distraction for the time being. We walk down the hall in silence until we turn the corner. I spot to Adam talking to Margie a few feet away. She was smiling trying her best to look cute. I grit my teeth as I feel a ping of jealously hit me hard.

"I told you he doesn't care about you." Slade says in an angry voice as he walks pass me to enter my classroom. What did I have to be jealous about? Adam wasn't mine and I wasn't his. He *was* fair game. Besides, with my dad being in the picture, we could never happen. I walk pass Adam as I enter my class only to hear Adam tell her that something was a serious matter and that she should take whatever they were talking about seriously. Hearing Adam sound serious like he always did with her, made me feel better because I knew for sure they weren't talking about what I assumed them to be talking about. I sit down at my seat and listen to Slade argue with the teacher about taking ten points off of his paper because he turned it in late. When Slade left, Mr. Wake lectures us about how turning in late work will result in ten points being deducted from our grade. After that wonderful lecture (note the sarcasm) we went into the lesson of the course. Chemical equations.

I'm not the best when it comes to math but I'm *certainly* not the worst. To say that it was hard was an understatement. After class I go to geometry. Wasn't it ironic how I start my first class off with math only to have math again? I smile and shake my head as I mentally laugh at myself.

"If that isn't a lovely smile, then I don't know what is." I hear Slade say beside me. My smile quickly fades off my face as I feel myself being snapped back to reality. I look over at him to see that he was looking at me with that same smirk he always wore. I roll my eyes which causes him to lightly chuckle.

"Alright," Ms. Nicks says as she unclips a stack of paper in her hands. She starts passing them to students telling them to take one and pass it down. "These are your study guides. At the end of every page are questions. Pages one and two will due be tomorrow at the beginning of class and the reason being is that, I have to leave early today and a substitute will take my place. I just wanted to explain to you all what you will be doing. You will have the rest of class to finish this assignment." When she's done passing out the papers, she sits at her desk and turns all her attention towards the computer. When I get my study guide, I stare at it. I couldn't work on this, not now or maybe not even tonight if I'm being honest. The only thing my mind was focused on, was the letter my mom wrote. Even though the envelope was sealed tight, some part of me says that my dad peeked inside and perfectly sealed it closed. I have no clue where he would learn to do that.

But then again, I have no idea what my dad does for a living. He always gone. Sometimes he's gone for days, weeks, and on rare occasions; months. The longest I'd ever been left alone was three months. They were the best three months of my life. Sometimes I miss those days because they helped me to calm down with everything going on in my life. Which isn't much besides getting abused by the one person who I can't deny as a relative. I sigh and bring my attention back to my study guide that is still blank. I look at the first question and my mind goes blank once again.

"The answer is 1.4555 repeated, but just to keep it simple, use two significant figures. So, 1.5." I hear Slade say. I look over at him and it takes me a second to realize what he was telling me. "The answer, beautiful is 1.5." He repeats once more winking at me.

"I think I'll just do my own work, but if I have any questions I'll let you know." I write on my notebook paper. I hand him the paper and watch him read it. He chuckles as his eyes meet mine. "That's cute love, really it is but I am smart. I may not *look* the part but trust me when I say this; the things I know, would blow your mind." Slade says. He then went back to his study guide to finish, leaving me stuck.

"Things like what?" I write to him as I let my curiosity get the best of me. He chuckles when he reads the paper. He looks over at me before he speaks

"Okay, I'll let you have this one. I know how to fix motorcycles. I even *own* one. In fact, if you want a car, if and when you get your license if you don't already have one which I'm betting you don't since Hollywood boy over there gives you rides and stuff, then you let me know." Slade says all in one breath. "Oh, and I almost forgot," Slade says as he tears a small piece of paper out his notebook. He writes something on it before handing it to me. "That, is my business card." He says as he stands up. The bell rings as he walks out the door. I look at the paper and it had his number on it and underneath his number it says "feel free to call me beautiful. I'm never too busy, especially for you." I roll my eyes as I began to gather my things. As I find my way to my locker, I see Adam leaning against the locker next to mine. In one hand, he held his books while his other hand was in his pocket. He slightly pushes himself off the locker once he spots me. He greets me with that killer smile of his and I couldn't resist the smile that forms on my face.

"So, I was thinking, today's the weekend, and well normal people go hang out and if you haven't caught on yet, I'm pretty boring and normal is overrated." He says while lightly chuckling. You have no idea. "and we have a project and I wanted to know if you'd like to get started on that today. That is if there's not a family gathering or anything going on today." He said sounding a bit nervous.

I look at him and smirk at his nervousness. "What?" he asks confused. I shake my head. I shut my locker and walk towards the exit doors. Having him there would put my mind at ease with my mom's letter. I mean I'll have to deal with it eventually but not right now. I have other important things to do, plus having Adam wouldn't be like asking for a death wish because my dad wouldn't be home.

"I-is that a yes or..." Adam trails off. I nod my head. "Okay, I'll bring the car around." He says while smiling. I watch as he jogs into the parking lot. I wait on the sidewalk as Adam goes to fetch his car. I was very nervous seeing that Adam's never been inside my house and it didn't help that we would be alone. My heart thrashes in my chest when realization kicks in. Maybe this was a bad idea. I could back out, it wasn't too late. I could go inside the school and hide right now. I take a deep breath as I find myself fiddling with my fingers.

"It's gonna be fine. We're going get started on this packet and everything will be fine." I mentally tell myself. A few seconds go by and Adam pulls up to the curve. He gets out and opens the door for me. "After you." He says. I get in and we take off. The ride was quiet except for the air condition coming through the vents of his car. When we approach my street, I make Adam park six houses down from mine. If my dad just happened to come back, there wouldn't be a car for him to see and I could always hide Adam.

"I'm guessing your parents won't take it lightly if they come home and find you with a guy in your room. That could look different to a lot of people." Adam says as we walk to my house.

When we get there, I unlock the door.

"Here goes nothing." I mentally tell myself. He closes the door behind us, locking it. "Wow, I take back what I was thinking in my head the first time I dropped you off." He says. This causes me to look back at him. "You guys have made a lot some changes to the house. I mean, the floors are no longer carpet and the walls...It's nice to have a change every once in a while." He says while looking around. I'd rather not talk about any of the changes that were made. I point to the ceiling as if to say "upstairs."

"Right." Adam says as he follows me upstairs. My bedroom door was slightly ajar. I open it and Adam enters after me. He chuckles lightly. I turn and look at him. He points to my stuffed animal infested shelf.

"I didn't take you for a stuffed animal collector." He says as he approaches my shelf. "But then again, I have a pretty nice collection of action figures myself so..." he trails off while smiling at me.

He turns his attention back to looking at my shelf. I smile and shake my head. He spots the picture of my mom and me. "I remember this picture. We went to Disney World." Adam says while smiling. He was there? I shake my head as a confused expression takes over my face. "I was in that same store as you but I was with my parents and I saw your dad taking a picture of you and your mom. That was a really good day." Adam explains. Yeah it was a good day. That's my favorite picture of my mom and I together. I feel the tears form in my eyes. I turn away which causes Adam to turn his attention to me. "Hey." He says as he starts to approach me. I couldn't stop the tears from falling down my face. He didn't say anything else after that, he just gave me a comforting hug and let me silently sob. Why couldn't she have just stayed here for me. Why didn't she just come back for me? Why did she leave me here with the monster I call my father? Why me? Why? "It's okay, you're okay." Adam says comforting me. I hate that my life was the way it was. Once I calm down, I pull away from Adam and go to the bathroom to blow my nose. I wash my hands and splash my face with cold water. This was my way of pulling it together. Adam looks at me with a sad expression. "Annabelle, we don't have to do our project. We can talk about whatever made you upset." Adam offers. I shake my head and sat on the floor next to my backpack. Adam mimics me as he pulls out his folder and a pencil. I pull out my laptop as well as my packet and a pencil.

"One day my dad and I came home from Dairy Queen and my mom left a note practically saying she was leaving us. After that day, we never saw her again. Sometimes looking at that picture just makes me sad." I write to him. He was now the only person outside the family to know about my mom. Adam reads the note and I watch as his mouth opens slightly as he was surprised and sad at the news I was delivering to him. It was nice to be able to talk to someone about this. Maybe this could help take some of the pain away. He looks up at me.

"Annabelle, I...I had no idea. I'm so sorry." He says. I wave my hand to tell him not to apologize to me. The room falls quiet while he just looks at me. I didn't want to talk about this anymore. I start working on our project not even acknowledging his gaze. He gets the idea shortly after because he begins to work on his part. An hour passes by and the room is filled with the clicking of keyboards. I look up at Adam to see his eyes glued to the screen. There was one thing poking at my brain.

"Who is that Asian lady in your sketch book?" I write to Adam. He chuckles a bit.

"She was a babysitter for us, well, for me. When both of our parents had to work, your parents would drop you off at my house. I happened to have a babysitter. Her name was Katherine Jay." Adam explains. I knew I had seen her somewhere before. I couldn't understand why I'd have a dream about someone who babysat me years ago. And why would he have a drawing of her? Adam grabs his phone.

"Do you like pizza?" He asks out of nowhere. I nod my head. "What about pepperoni?" He asks.

I nod my head.

"Why?" I mouth to him.

"Good," he says, ignoring my question. "Because I just ordered some." I shake my head smiling. Adam smiles. "And there's that beautiful smile that went away for a while." I roll my eyes and he chuckles. You know this actually wasn't bad at all. I'm actually glad I chose to spend this day with Adam. He always knew the right things to say to me to get me to smile. Even before my mom left, it was always Adam who cheered me up. He was the only one who could.

"I wish you hadn't moved away when my mom left us. I needed someone who knew me to be there for me, someone who wasn't my dad who works all the time." I write to him.

"I won't leave you again. We're gonna walk across that stage together Annabelle, I promise." He says looking at me. I give him a small smile. "Plus, there wouldn't be a graduation if I weren't there. Come on now." He says being conceited. I roll my eyes at him and he chuckles. When the pizza got here, Adam and I reminisced on memories we shared up until we couldn't. Adam takes the last sip of his water as I take a sip of mine. "Annabelle, I've been thinking a lot." He says sounding a bit nervous. I look at him. "About you, I mean." He says while looking at me this time. I feel my heart flutter. He rubs the back of his neck. "I know we haven't seen each-other for a long time, but I've always liked you. Even before I moved away and it killed me that I couldn't be around you. That I couldn't hear your laugh, see that pretty smile or your beautiful face. I missed everything about you and now that you're here...I just wanna make this year count." He says. Talk about being stuck. I didn't know what to do or what I should say. I mean I like him too but I had no idea that he still felt this way about me. I feel the endless waves of butterflies in the pit of my stomach as I think about us being more than friends. He moved closer to me and moves a stray of hair behind my ear. Those endless waves of butterflies increase as I see him lean in to kiss me. I lean in too. I can't believe this is happening! He's going to kiss *me*! This'll be the highlight of my night. He places his hand on the right side of my face as his warm soft lips touch mine. Our lips move in sync and for the first time in my life, there was nothing going on in my mind. I couldn't think and I didn't want to. I just want to enjoy this moment. We both pull away when we feel the need to breathe. We rest our foreheads together. "Annabelle." Adam says as we both caught our breaths. He opens his mouth to speak again but is interrupted when I hear the stairs creak. I stand up abruptly and Adam looks at me confused.

"Wha-" Adam begins to speak but I put my finger to my lips. Adam stands up and I quickly grab his belongings. I put them in his backpack before handing them to him. That couldn't have been my dad, I mean he wasn't supposed to be home for a couple of days. I quickly guide Adam to the closet and push him in. I look at him to see a mixture of confusion and shock written on his face as I close the door. I go back over to where we sat to make sure I didn't miss anything but when I make my way over to our spot, the door opens. To say I was beyond scared would be an understatement. I was so scared I felt like I was going to pass out. I stand still as the intruder reveals himself as my dad. He looks at me standing in the middle of my room. I see his eyes drift down at the pizza box on the floor. He scoffs before his eyes meet mine.

"When you're finished, I need you to fix dinner, unfortunately I missed the train thanks to you and had to wait several hours for my guys to bring my truck back. But you wouldn't know anything about that, now would you? You little..." he trails off as he looks at what I'm guessing was the pizza box. The next few words he says to me makes my blood run cold. "Why are there two plates?" he asks me sounding upset. I was so worried about Adam I didn't bother to hide the most obvious thing. The hairs on my neck stand up and at this point I'm surprised they didn't jump off my neck and hide. I swallow, my mouth feeling dry. "Annabelle," He presses. "You didn't have a boy over here, did you? Because we had a nice little chat about that weeks ago. Do you remember what I said to you?" He asks. I nod my head vigorously. "So, I will ask you again, did you have a boy in this house?" he asks. I shake my head. "So, it was a girl?" he asks and I nod my head. "What was her name?" He asks me. I quickly grab a piece of paper. I write down the first name that comes to me. "Mariette?" He asks once reading the name I wrote down. I nod my head hoping he would buy it but something told me he wouldn't. "Huh..." he trails off and the look he had on his face told me he didn't believe me. "Well, you tell Mariette, that she can no longer come over here. I told you I don't want anybody in this house and especially when I'm not here." He says and with that he slams my door. I stand still as I shake out of fear. I listen to him walk down the hall. I then hear the bath tub running. I let out a shaky breath as I close my eyes. The closet door opens slowly causing me to open my eyes. I forgot Adam was even here for a second.

"Wow, your dad is a jerk. He was never like this before." He says quietly. Jerk isn't even the word I would use to describe him. I quickly grab Adam's hand and lead him to my door. He stops me. "I can jump from the terrace." He says. I look at him with a "Are you crazy?" look. "Annabelle, I've jumped from higher. I promise. Okay, clearly your dad is upset and if he catches you trying to sneak me out, you and I both know that will only make matters worse." He says.

"You have no idea." I mentally think. We walk to my terrace and I open the door and Adam walks out with me taking my hand in his.

"Thank you for tonight. I wish it could have gone better without our interruption but you can't always have your cake and eat it too." He says as he gives me a quick peck on the lips and then on my nose. "I'll see you tomorrow." He says smiling while letting going of my hand. I smile back and give him a small wave. He swings one leg over the terrace and then the other. He looks at me once more before jumping off.

"Annabelle!" I hear my dad yell which makes me jump. He was standing behind me. My breathing increases and I brace myself for the beating I was gonna get in front of Adam but it never came. "I thought I made it clear you had 30 minutes to get down there and make my food." He says with his hands on either side of him. I nod my head quickly and he walks out. He never mentioned 30 minutes...jerk. I take a quick glance in my room to see my door shut and I walk out on the terrace to see Adam running through our front yard and to the side walk. I smile as I watch him run. Maybe this could work, maybe we *could* be together. I sigh as I go to the kitchen and think of what I'll cook for him. I pull out two eggs, milk, pancake batter, and bacon. He'll have breakfast for dinner tonight. It's the only thing that is easy for me to cook. I put the bacon in first and then I start on the pancake batter. When I was finished with everything, my dad's voice startles me which causes me to jump. He was sitting down in the chair in his favorite flannel sleep pants and the white shirt he was wearing when mom left.

"Breakfast for dinner?" he chuckles. "You aren't making me breakfast because I made you breakfast, are you? he asks while letting out a chuckle. I shrug as I began fixing his plate. I jump once I feel the presence of my dad standing right behind me. He sniffs me. The next thing he said made me want to pee my pants. "You were with a boy up there." He says in a deadly tone. I shake my head only to stop when he slams his hands on the counter next to me.

"Don't! Lie to me! I smell cologne and I know you don't wear cologne let alone perfume. I'm sure this "Mariette" or whoever, didn't wear perfume and even if she did," he pauses for a few seconds. "It wouldn't be on you. So, I'm gonna ask you one more time, was there a boy up there?" He asks. I swallow and shake my head. Without warning, I feel a hot sting on the side of my face. He hit me so hard that I fell on the floor. "You're gonna sit here and lie straight to my face?" he asks me. I can hear the anger in his voice. My eyes start to water. He crouches down and slaps me again. Something warm runs down my nose and I didn't dare move. He stays in a crouched position as he spits hurtful words to my face. "I have tried so hard to make this work you little delinquent...And I've come to realize why this isn't working. It's because you're nothing to me...you're not my daughter, you're not family, you're a waste of space...a mistake that I'm going to fix." he says to me. He stands up and stomps hard on my ankle. It snaps and I release a sound I haven't made for a very long time...I scream.

Chapter 14

Adam approached his car with a smile on his face. He leaned on the driver's side door and looked up at the black sky. He had just kissed and confessed his feelings to the only girl he's had feelings for. The best part for him, was that she had feelings for him too. The only problem would be keeping secrets from her. He stays like that for a moment, reminiscing the kiss he shared with Annabelle. Before he could do anything else, he hears what sounds like a scream. Panic rises in him as he thinks it might have come from Annabelle's house. He quickly darts towards her house and climbs his way onto her terrace with the aid from one of the trees branches that leaned towards her room. The door wasn't closed all the way, so he makes his way inside. He looks around the room as the sound of running water fills his ears.

"You made me do this! Everything I've done to you, you asked me for it!" Adam hears Annabelle's dad shout. He didn't waste time as he followed the sound. He approached the bathroom first and the sight he took in made his blood run cold. He growls as his canines elongate from his gums.

"What are you—" Annabelle's dad starts but is cut off when Adam roars at him. Annabelle was faced first in the tub filled with water and her body was limp. Her dad let go of Annabelle and stands up quick. Without warning he tackles Adam into the hallway and rolls on top of him. He wraps his hand around Adam's neck and attempts to choke Adam but Adam head butts him and he lets go. Using his strength, Adam pushes Annabelle's dad off of him and he flies into the blue wall. A few blue chips of paint on the wall fall onto Annabelle's dad. Adam growls as he slowly stalks towards him. Adam's claws began to extend as he closes in for the kill. Annabelle's dad gets up and runs towards Adam in attempt to get away, but Adam catch him by the neck and shoves him down the stairs. He tumbles down the stairs and his head makes hard contact with the floor. His eyes close immediately and he doesn't move. Adam growls and almost goes to finish him off but the sound of the running water reminds him of what was more important. He quickly approaches Annabelle as he turns to his normal self. He quickly and gently pulls her out and lays her on the white tiles of the bathroom floor. Adam takes in her injuries. She had blood on the side of her forehead, and bruises both her arms and legs. The biggest bruise she had was on her ankle and Adam keeps in mind that it might be broken.

"I shouldn't have left you. I should've stayed, I'm so sorry Annabelle." Adam says as tears form in his eyes. His heart begins to beat faster as fear rises in him when he realizes she wasn't breathing. "No, No, No. This is not how it ends for you, for us." He says as he starts giving her CPR. He blows air into her lungs and starts doing chest compressions. "Come on Annabelle!" Adam says getting frustrated that she wasn't responding. Annabelle's eyes open as she starts coughing up water. Adam pulls her in a hug as he cries. "I th-thought you were gonna die." He sobs as he continues to hold her and kiss her the top of her head. Annabelle doesn't say anything, she only closes her eyes. He gently picks her up and takes her to the only place he knew she would be safe.

Chapter 15

I know I'm laying down on something soft but I can't open my eyes. The softness of the bed was nothing like the one at the hospital, and it certainly wasn't my bed. Where was I and what happened? I can only remember Adam and I sharing our first kiss. That beautiful moment (that I'll probably never experience again) being squashed my dad showing up. I also recall being forced into a tub filled with ice cold water and from there my mind goes blank. I try to open my eyes again but they won't budge. I then try to move and that's just as much of an epic fail as opening my eyes.

"You have to eat, or at least sleep. You haven't done any of those things." A masculine voice says.

"Like I said two hours ago, I'm not eating or sleeping until she wakes up." I hear Adam reply in a stern voice that reminds me of my dad. Wait, Adam? What's going on? "I have to be here when she opens her eyes...I have to be." I hear Adam say again, his voice growing soft. I try to open my eyes but they still won't budge.

"I get it. Really, I do but you won't be much help to her if you're not in good shape yourself. Come on man,

I'll take watch. At least shower or move around. You've been sitting in the same spot for five days, Adam. How—" The person says but is cut off by Adam.

"I said no!" Adam growls out. Wait, growls? Is my hearing off?

"You're gonna have to try better than that if you want me to back down. Plus, your mom said for you to rest." the person says.

"Luke, how many times do I have to tell you and everyone in this house. I said no!" Adam says a little louder. I hear Luke sigh.

"Fine." Luke says and a few seconds I hear the door open and close.

"Come on Annabelle. I know you'll wake up soon, you have to Bee. I can't...If you don't wake soon, I don't know what I'll do..." He trails off, his voice soft. He sounded like he was on the verge of tears. It was like his words were magic because that's when I opened my eyes. I blink a couple of times as I adjust to the environment. Out of the corner of my eye, I see Adam was sitting in a chair right beside me. Adam inches closer to me.

"Annabelle?" Adam says as he touches my hand lightly. I look over at him and he smiles bit. He had blood shot eyes and he looked like he was due for a nap very soon. "How are you feeling? Do you...do you want anything? How about water? Does water sound okay?" he asks ambushing me with questions. Water does sound nice. I nod my head and he goes over to the dresser in front of the bed. He begins pouring water from a pitcher into the glass cup. I take in my surroundings. I wasn't in a hospital like I had predicted, in fact I was in someone's room. Not that I'm complaining, the room is spacious. The walls are grey with two big mirrors on the wall. There was one in between two windows in front of the bed and the other was on my left side. On my right, I see one wide window and next to that window was a terrace. Through the sheer orangish-red curtains, I could see a garden. There was a big dresser with a TV built in it. I wish I had one of those, but then again what would I do with a TV? I look up at the white ceiling to find a miniature chandelier. I would be the happiest person in the world if I had a room like this one. "Here you go, but small sips, okay?" Adam says while handing the cup to me. When I reach out to get it, I groan as my body aches. "Why don't you just let me do everything for you." Adam suggests. I shake my head in protest. I grab the cup despite the pain I feel and take a sip. I feel refreshed once the ice-cold water fills my sandpaper mouth. I finish within seconds. I hand it back to Adam and he chuckles.

"More?" he asks.

"Yes please" I thought as I nod my head. I then notice that my left ankle was hoisted up and it was in a cast. My foot couldn't have been broken, I mean I'm a clumsy person, but I've never broken a bone. Adam must've noticed me looking at my leg when he turned around because he spoke.

"Your ankle's broken." he says while handing the cup to me. He doesn't sound too happy. I mean who would? I gulp the water ice-cold water down in seconds. "There are no words to describe how angry I am at what he did to you. He's been hurting you all this time, hasn't he?" he asks, and I can't help but feel ashamed at hiding the truth from him. "The bruises that you said were from the fall at the field...It was..." He shakes his head and turns away from me while running a hand through his hair.

"They were all lies." He says in a low tone. He couldn't be mad at me because anyone in my position would do the same. Especially if the lives of those they cared about were threatened. "Why didn't you tell me Bee? I would've helped you." He says as he turns around and faces me. He grabs my hands in his. "Annabelle, I' am your friend, more than your friend. You can come to me for and about anything. I will always protect you. Always." Adam says. Just then the door opens and a tall boy walks in. He looks to be about thirteen.

"Your mom needs you." The boy says. Adam looks at me and then back at the boy.

"Keep her company for me." Adam orders as he walks out the door. The boy smiles lightly at me and sits in a chair on the sides of me.

"I'm Hemingway, they call me "Ming" for short." Well this is awkward because I can't do anything but stay silent. "It's okay, I know about you and the not talking thing. It must be really awkward for you at times huh?" He asked. I nod my head and smile. Ming and I got to know each-other with him asking me yes or no questions and him telling me about himself. He reminds me of my cousin Brendon. My cousin had a round face and Ming's was more oval shaped. He was quite chatty like my cousin and the freckles on his face didn't help. The only difference between the two was that Brendon had brown hair and Ming had dirty blonde hair. Ming had his hair cut like the brothers from *"The suite life of Zack and Cody"*. I never understood why some boys like that style. It makes their heads look like mushrooms.

"Are you and Adam like a thing?" he asks after a few moments of awkward silence between us. Oh, wow...I didn't see *that* coming. I'd like to think of us as being a couple, not a thing. I mean it was established last night, but I need to focus on what was going on. I didn't know how to answer that. I feel my face heat up as I look at him. He holds a smirk on his face as he folds his arms. His eyebrows wiggle and if I could laugh aloud at this kid, I would be laughing right now. I smile and shake my head. "I knew it! You like Adam." he teased. Oh gosh, how did I get here. After a few minutes of him trying to get me to admit my feelings for Adam, the door opens and Adam steps inside carrying a tray of food. He smiles as he sees me smiling and Ming laughing.

"You guys sound too happy without me." Adam says in a joking matter.

"It was nice meeting you Annabelle. "Ming says as he gets off the chair and walks towards the door. He winks at me before he closes the door. I smile and shake my head at him. That little boy is something else.

"Sorry about him. He can be a bit too much at times, but I knew he'd make you smile. If anything, that's one thing he's good for." he says as gets closer to me. "Hungry yet?" Adam asks. I nod my head. "I figured. I mean, being out cold for five days will do that to you." He says jokingly. I reach my hands out thinking he's going to give me the tray but he shakes his head. I give him a confused look. "I'm going to feed you." He says. What am I? A baby? I shake my head in protest. "Annabelle, really it's okay. I'm here for you so let me be here for you." He says. I sigh after a few more protest and nod my head in agreement. He picks up the fork. "Now, we have steak, green beans, and mashed potatoes. Which would you like first. 1, 2, or 3?" he asks. I put up one finger and he cut the steak for me and brings a piece to my mouth. Whoever cooked this deserves an "A plus" because this is the most delicious steak I have ever tasted in my life. After he was done feeding me he gave me a composition book and a pen. I look up at him. "I know you have questions and I'm willing to answer them." He says with a serious face. He sat down in the chair that was beside me.

"How did I end up here. And where is *here* exactly?" I write to him.

"Well, I was going to go home and I heard you scream and I went in and," he pauses, clearly having a hard time reaching back into the event that took place a few days ago. "He was drowning you Bee. I thought...I thought I was too late..." He says. I could see the pain behind his eyes as his eyebrows furrow. I didn't know how I felt about hearing this. I knew this day would come eventually, I just didn't know that I would have my own knight in shining armor come to my rescue.

"And my dad?" I write to him.

"I pushed him down the stairs," He pauses. "But he'll live." He says as if he didn't want him to and I don't blame him. "Oh, and here is my home." He adds.

"Thank you, this means a lot to me." I write to him.

"Don't thank me. It's my job to have your back." He says.

"Back to that night, what exactly happened to you? How were you able to get up the next day?" I write to him. Adam shifts in his seat.

"One of my friends had picked a bone with a group of guys who sold parts for motorcycles and he owed them a fair amount of money. He was supposed to pay them back but he didn't. They didn't like that so they followed him home on his walk from work. They chased him in a warehouse and luckily, he was able to hide but they were three of them. He called me and I came. Little did I know, they had guns and started to shoot up the place. I was hiding just like my friend but the only problem was that the bullets were bouncing off of things, and that's how some got me. Eventually my friend and I were to get away but in doing so we got separated," Adam pauses. "But somehow through all of that, I found you. I wasn't looking for you in particular, your house just happened to be the one I stopped at.

Annabelle, you saved my life." Adam explains. That still didn't explain how he was okay the next few days.

"You never answered my question about how you were okay and at school." I write to him. I didn't mean to sound like I wanted him to die, it's just it seems impossible...it *is* impossible.

"I got lucky, I guess." Adam says. He got lucky? What kind of answer is that? He's lying to me. He was now putting the food tray on the dresser.

"If you were a demon, you would tell me, right?" I write to him. Afraid of his answer I was a bit hesitant to let him read what I wrote.

Adam looks at the paper, then at me, and bursts out in laughter. He was laughing so hard his face turned red. I put on my serious face and he sobers up with a few snickers in between. He wipes his teary eyes.

"Yes, I would if I were." He replies.

"How do I know that everything you're telling me isn't a lie?" I write to him.

"Because I'm giving you a chance to ask whatever you want. Which means, I'm to tell you everything you want. The incident with my friend was the truth.

The warehouse wasn't close to your house. I traveled a pretty good distance, in case they were following me. I ran for my life Bee. I don't think I've ever been that terrified in my life. But after you fixed me up, the next morning my friend gave me a call and picked me up. As for the healing part, my dad makes medicine from herbs and when his father fought in Vietnam he had that same medicine. It would help to close wounds faster to prevent infection. It's like pouring salt on your tongue when you have a cut. Minus the burning of course." He explains. He then starts unbuttoning his shirt and out of instinct I look away. I hear him chuckle. "Relax, I'm not going to strip bare in front of you. I'm giving you proof about the herbs. I mean there's no way I could heal like that after a gunshot wound." He says. He slips his arms out of the blue flannel long sleeve. On his torso, I see the bullet wounds that I pulled the bullets out of. The scars were only a little dark. The one that was right above his heart looked newer than the rest. I let my eyes wander as I take in his appearance, and my oh my, he was ripped! My eyes travel down to his six-pack abs. He must work out every day for that. I was totally ogling at his beautiful body. He clears his throat and my eyes find their way up to his face, which held a smirk.

"Are you done checking me out?" he asks. I turn away instantly feeling hot on my face. "Believe me now?" he asks. I did believe him about the wounds but not about the other stuff he told me. I know that there's more to the story than he's letting on but what can I do about that? When he's ready, maybe he'll tell me.

"What happened between you and Slade? I remember he went to your birthday party when we were younger." I write to him, trying to change the subject.

"When I moved away, I moved right next door to Slade. We went to the same school and everything. We were cool back then but that all changed when he thought he dominated everyone in that school. My aunt had died that day and I was just having the worst moment in my life. He came in and tried to push me around and I wasn't having it so we got in a fight. Ever since then, we've been at this back and forth thing." Adam explains. He had an expression that I've never seen before; guilt. He stands up and his facial expression changes as he smiles at me. "Do you want a tour of the Vere estate?" he offers. Well it beats being in bed all day. I nod my head and he gently leg lays my leg down. "I'll be back in a second." He says as he leaves the room without. He comes back rather fast wheeling in a wheel chair. He helps me get seated in the wheel chair and we go out into the blue hallway. The hallway was long, like one in a hotel and the ceilings were white and high. They were a few rooms that we passed every few feet. Maybe we were in a hotel, but didn't he say...the Vere estate? He wheels me to an elevator. Wait an elevator? This has to be a hotel because who on earth has an elevator in their own home? When the doors open we get in and I notice there were only three buttons labeled one to three. "We're on the third floor in case you're wondering." Adam says as he presses button number one. It becomes awkward, once the doors close. It was so quiet that I couldn't even feel the presence of Adam standing behind me. If this wasn't a hotel...maybe I'm in a mansion. If his parents can afford an elevator in their house, then that must mean his parents have lots of mula.

Imagine that, how did someone like me end up with a rich guy? The odds of that happening aren't even listed. Maybe Adam and I *will* get married. My mom always said to marry a man who can provide for his family. I mentally laugh at myself. I collect my thoughts when the elevator "dings" indicating that we'd reached our destination. He wheels me out of the hallway and I'm greeted by a bright pretty orange wall.

"Adam! Come and let us meet with Annabelle! I know you're down here!" a feminine voice yells.

"Can I get her warmed up first so you all don't scare her away?" Adam says jokingly. I was nervous because if this is Adam's parents' house then that means I'm more likely to see them. I haven't seen them in years. I didn't know what to expect. "I'm sorry about that. It's just my mom's been a real pain about seeing you since you got in." Adam explains as he pushes me around the corner. The first thing I see is a dark green marbled floor. The steps of the stairs are green and the wooden railing is dark brown. It wrapped around the big chandelier that hung in the middle. This was like something you'd see in a movie. I hear distinct talking that echoed throughout the house. As we continue to pass the staircase I take note of the type of style his house was. This was a manor house. I know this because a couple of summers ago, I went to England to stay with my aunt. She had a manor house and the way Adam's house was set up, put me in the mind of her. If only I could see her and tell her the horrible things that have happened. Come to think of it, no one's spoken to us since my mom left. It's almost as if my mom's side of the family is shunning us. My dad never spoke of his family so it's not like that mattered anyway. Adam comes around in front of me snapping me out of my thoughts and opens a glass door. Wait glass door? Holy marshmallows! First it was the elevator and now it's a glass door? What's next and indoor swimming pool? Man, maybe I should ask to hold a few grand sometime. I mentally laugh at myself. The glass door leads to the living room which was quite spacious as the rest of the house (at least the parts I'd seen). There were a good number of people who were standing around conversing with one another like a family reunion. I only see two kids, a boy and a girl chasing each-other.

"Johnathan! Claire! You know there is no running in here." Adam says making them stop.

"Yes, uncle Adam." Johnathan and Claire say sounding bummed out. Adam's an uncle? That must mean he has siblings. I never knew he had siblings. He pushes me over to a white couch and helps me sit on it. This couch is nothing like the one I have at home. Home... It just dawned on me that I haven't been home for...well for five days. When I come back home, my dad is going to finish the job and kill me. I'm going to get the worst beating of my life. Adam must've seen the panicked expression on my face because he was in front of me crouched down looking me in the eyes.

"Hey, hey, what's wrong?" he asks. I notice my breathing was picking up. Every time I breathed it felt like it wasn't enough. Oh god, I'm having a panic attack and everyone's gonna see me. Adam put his hands on both of my shoulders. "Annabelle, I need you to focus on my voice. Can you do that for me?" He says sounding calm. I close my eyes as I start to feel dizzy from all the short breaths I was taking. He continues to talk to me and eventually I got a hold of myself. He gave me some water and sits next to me. "I know this is a lot to take in, but I didn't know where else to take you. My parents have a mutual friend who's a doctor and so I thought maybe bringing you here would mean it'd be safer for you." He explains. I understand why he did what he did and if I were in his shoes I would probably do the same for him. Me being here wasn't the problem, it was just me being here for so long. Wouldn't the school have questioned my absence? We are only allowed to miss up to 4 days, unless there is some significant reason why we aren't at school.

"Oh, my goodness, Annabelle. It's been so long. You are more beautiful than what Adam said you were!" I hear a woman say in excitement. Before I can turn to look at her she embraces me in a hug I froze. She pulls back and apologizes for being all over me. When I look at her, I smile. This was Verna, Adam's mom. She was wearing a black dress with heels to match and red lipstick. I watch her as she smiles at me. Her eyes analyze my face. "You've grown to be a beautiful young lady...Gosh, you look so much like your mother..." She trails off still looking at me like I'm the greatest thing since bread. I swallow as I feel a lump in my throat at the mention of my mom. I see Adam's shoulders rise in the corner of my eye, as he draws in a breath. I guess what she said had caught him off guard too.

"Mom, you're going to scare her away and she's never gonna wanna come back." Adam says jokingly trying to change the subject. Instead of giving in to the sadness I was feeling, I simply smile.

"Just ignore my pushy son. Gosh, are all guys in your age group like this?" she asks me. I hope she wasn't waiting for an answer, because it wasn't like I could give her one. I look over to Adam for help and he must've caught on because he explained me not being able to talk to his mom. "Oh, well that's okay. Just know that you're welcome here at any time. If you'll excuse me." She says before walking away to join another conversation.

"I'm sorry. I...she didn't know." He says apologetically. I shake my head in protest. It was okay, I need to move on anyway. After meeting his mom, other people introduce themselves to me. I discovered a few interesting things from the people who I met. In fact, today was Adam's 22nd family reunion. Every family member and friends traveled long distances just to be here today. These family reunions must be very special to them (especially if there's a money give away. In that case, I'd be here too, even if I lived in Japan). Adam has two older brothers and one sister. I like his sister Lexi. I could tell she was laid back and wasn't afraid to tell you where to stick it. I think her and I would get along just fine. His older brother Zeke, was scary. He seemed like the serious type. He didn't even smile when Adam made a joke, which I found to be funny. He only shrugged him off, but Adam didn't let it bother him. His second older brother, Ethan was a lot friendlier than Zeke. He didn't intimidate me like Zeke did.

"Alright! Settle down everyone!" Ethan yells in the room. He had brown curly hair that was almost messy, brown eyes, and a little stubble that clearly showed he had a beard. The room got quiet and everyone turns in my direction.

"Adam." Ethan says as he looks at him, then at me. He gives me a small smile and I return the smile back. Adam stands up and my attention is on him.

The people in the room stare at him. I catch a few eyes on me as well.

"As you all know, I brought a very special person here tonight. Some of you had the pleasure of meeting her and some didn't. For those who haven't, her name is Annabelle. The history her and I have, it's special. Very special." He said as he glances at me with that smile that always got me to smile. Where is he going with this? He turns back to the crowd.

"We were best friends growing up, the best of friends. Then I moved away and never thought I'd see her again, but somehow, some way we met again and I'm truly grateful for that. Annabelle is and will always be one of us. As of today, she is a part of this family and will be staying here for a while, so make our new family member feel lots of love and welcomed here." Adam says as everyone claps and flashes smiles my way. Who said I was staying? After the applauding crowd dies down, multiple conversations become the main source of noise in the room. Adam turns to me and I shoot him a look. He sits down next to me.

"I know we didn't talk about his but you'd be safer here." He says.

I wanted to reply to him but I didn't have my journal or a pencil for that matter. As if reading my mind, he hands me his phone.

"How do I know here is safe?" I type before handing him the phone.

"Because I won't let anything happen to you. I know you're afraid he'll come looking for you. Even if he did, he wouldn't find you. Think about it. What would he tell police? That I was abusing my daughter and was in the process of killing her until some boy came in and ran off with her." He says. I suppose he's right, but my father could easily lie. He could turn the tables around and make it seem like Adam was the one abusing me. If caught me and wanted Adam to pay he'd kill me for sure. Maybe I am better off here, wherever *here* is. I nod my head.

"So, you'll stay?" Adam asks slightly smiling. I nod my head once more and he smiles. But one thing hit my mind. What about school? "Great, you're really gonna love it here." Adam says smiling.

"Adam." I hear Zeke's deep voice say. I turn to see Zeke approaching us.

"Zeke if this is about the car—" Adam was cut off by Zeke.

"Father needs you for something. He's in the kitchen." Zeke says. Adam sighs.

"okay, watch her for me." Adam orders Zeke. Zeke sat next to me.

"Welcome home Annabelle," he says while smiling at me. I return a smile. He had gray eyes with brown hair that was buzz cut and a nicely tamed beard. They're all related but none of them have similar facial structures. I find that a bit bizarre.

"You're really going to like it here." He says. Just then a tall man, maybe about 6'1 came in. He had a brown beard that made him look like a lumber jack. (What's up with everyone having a beard?) He had greenish-hazel eyes and wore a black suit with a red tie. He looked very serious and I'm willing to bet that's where Zeke gets his seriousness from. His deep voice filled the room.

"Everyone, dinner is served!" he yells over the bickering crowd. Everyone in the room makes their way towards the exit. I spot Adam squeezing through people to get to me. When he reaches, me he smiles.

"Do you want a tour the rest of the house?" Adam asks. I nod and he helps me into the wheel chair and takes me to the elevators. This elevator was nicer than the first one we went in. I watch as Adam pushes a button that says "3B". I point to the button and turn halfway around to face him. "It's a place I go to when I need alone time. I think you'll like it." He says. When the elevator doors open, all that I see is a long white dim lit hallway. At the end of the hallway was a brown door. I couldn't help but get an uncomfortable feeling as he pushes me into the hallway. I feel like I'm visiting a mental asylum (I should probably never watch America Horror Story anymore). When we go inside the room, it was nothing I had ever seen. The room was like an enchanted forest. There were trees, plants, and grass. I look up and the ceiling was a dark purplish black and the glimmer of tiny lights that would twinkle every now and then reminded me of stars. This was beautiful. "Me, Zeke, Ethan, and my dad did this. At first, it was just an indoor butterfly house, but then we decided to make it seem a little bit more real for them." he says, just as a blue and black butterfly flies over us. He pushes me over to a tree that had pretty green and yellow leaves. He sits me on the grass and sits next to me. "I like coming here because it helps me think. Being here and seeing what I've accomplished with building this, it makes me feel like I can do anything." Adam explains. I could tell he was in love with this place. I graze my hand across the soft and cold grass. I look over at Adam who was laying down with his eyes closed as a cool breeze hit us. He looked happy and peaceful. I lay down and mimic him. That was how we spent the rest of the day.

Chapter 16

My eyes snap open as I hear a soft knock on the door. I notice my foot is in a boot resting on a pillow. I was in the same room as before. I sit up slowly just as the door opens. I see Lexi poke her head in.

"I didn't wake you, did I?" she asks with concern. I shake my head. It was a good thing that I was up. Being a guest in their home didn't mean I could sleep the whole day. She opens the door and I see her carrying a tray of food. There were eggs, toast, and bacon with orange juice. I position myself against the back board of the bed. She hands me the plate and I waste no time in feasting. This is some of the best meals I've eaten in days. I should ask them about their recipe because not even my food tastes this good. When I finish, I hand her the plate. "Well, someone was hungry." She says and I blush a bit feeling embarrassed. "How's the foot?" she asks. I tilt my hand from side to side to tell her that it was okay. "Do you want pain medicine?" she asks. I shake my head. It was only a dull aching pain and a throbbing sensation. Plus, I've felt more pain than this before. "Okay, but if you do need some, don't be afraid to ask." She says as she places my plate on the dresser. She sits down in one of the chairs. What is up with them watching me? I'm not a child. I see my journal on the dresser beside me and I reach to grab it.

"Nope! I got it!" Lexi says as she runs over to get my journal and pencil.

"You don't have to watch me." I write to her.

"Adam wants me to. You are family now Annabelle. We look after each-other." She says.

"I don't get it. Do you guys not trust me or something?" I write her.

"Annabelle, I promise this has nothing to do with not trusting you. We just want to make a good impression." She explains.

"Shouldn't I be the one worrying about making a good impression?" I write to her. She chuckles.

"Well since you're going to be staying for a while, we don't want you to ever feel uncomfortable around any of us. This is good for us to watch you especially since you're injured. There's only so much you can do and we want to be here for you." She says. I guess that's somewhat of a reasonable answer but they shouldn't feel they have to buy their way into me liking them.

"Just be the real you. You shouldn't feel that you have to buy your way into me liking you guys. Plus, I think you're pretty cool as it is." I write to her. I watch as her face light up as her eyes skim the words on the page.

"Really?" she asks looking up at me. I nod my head. "Thanks Annabelle. This really means a lot, especially coming from you. You're the only girl my age and well, to be honest, you're actually the closest thing I have to a friend." She says. Okay, where are the cameras? Please tell me she's joking right now. She's never had friends? What? Her pretty dark brown hair that cascades down to her elbow and green eyes would leave a guy on his knees for her. She was pretty. Why wouldn't she have any friends? She seems like the type of girl to be popular with the crowds in school.

"Same thing goes for me too." I write to her.

"What?" she asks surprised as she looks at me with disbelief. "You're not being serious, are you?" she asks and I nod my head. I then get a feeling that I only ever get with Adam; trust. I didn't know why I felt I could trust her, but I did. This led to me telling her everything that's happened to me. After I told her my story, tears were streaming down her face like a water fall. While I was telling her how I got here, I swear I heard her growl, but I let it go. I was probably hearing things (which isn't a surprise). "That isn't fair. No one should have to go through something like that. No one." She says as she sniffles. I too was crying. Sharing those horrible things done to me was like reliving those events. "You don't have to ever worry about going back to that place ever again. We won't let him hurt you again Annabelle. I promise." She says. She gets up from the chair and sit on the edge of the bed. "Something I've never shared with anyone; I'm adopted. Adam's parents adopted me when I was fifteen. My dad was never really around because my parents got a divorce when I was about 8 or nine. So, my dad came into the picture once my mom passed away. He was never over the fact that she divorced him so he was still upset and when she died he became so mean to me. He made me feel so unwanted and so unloved. One day he tried to hurt and I stabbed with a knife and he hit me and the next thing I knew I was on the side of a highway in the middle of nowhere.

Adam's mom happened to be on that highway that night and she took me in. Ever since then I've been nothing less than family to everyone. They showed me what love is supposed to be like. What it's supposed to *feel* like. And What I've learned most in this family, is that this family lives on a code that no matter what we protect our own, and you Annabelle, you are one of us." She says. I would not have guessed that Lexi and I would have a similar background story. One look at her and you'd assume that everything was going right in her life. A tear rolls down my face as she pulls me in for a hug. We stay like that until we calm down. She pulls away and gives me a sad smile.

"Adam's nephew, Johnathan is having a 6th birthday party and I was wondering if you were up to coming? We'd really love it if you could come along with us. It'd be a great chance to get to know everyone" she offers. I nod my head and she smiles. "Okay, I'll be right back." She says as she excuses herself. Within minutes, she comes back with a pair of skinny black jeans and a cute grey shirt with black and white converse. I give her a look. "These are some clothes I got you. There's no doubt that you won't fit into these. I have a sharp eye." She says as she places then on the edge of the bed. She leaves the room for me to change and to my surprise, the clothes fit me well. She brings my wheel chair in and takes me downstairs to wait on everyone else to get ready. We end up having the party at a park where the children could run around and play. There were picnic blankets laid out for everyone to sit on and a lot of picnic baskets. I look around for Adam but he wasn't here. It was hard for me to concentrate on everyone else. When it came time for us to eat, Adam still wasn't here. I wonder where he was. I was currently sitting on a red blanket while listening to Lexi tell me about her experience with getting her first job. I hear a familiar masculine voice clear their throat. I turn around and my eyes land on Adam. He was wearing a white shirt, brown Sperry's, and khaki pants.

"Adam." Lexi says greeting him.

"Lexi, my dear sister." Adam greets her back, but his eyes never leave mine. There was a light smirk on his face.

"So, what have you been up to?" Lexi asks Adam as he sits down next to me, his eyes now on her.

"Nothing much, just handling things around the house. What about you? How's work going for you? Is that guy still trying to talk to you?" He asks her. I wonder if that's where he gets his protectiveness from?

"Work is fine and no. He doesn't even look my way thanks to you." Lexi says.

"Good. Because I don't want him to break your heart because you're so boring." Adam says jokingly.

"Hey!" Lexi says as she playfully pushes him.

"I am so sorry you had to spend time with her. I can only imagine how horrible it was." Adam jokes again. I smile and shake my head while Lexi rolls her eyes at him.

"If anything, she likes me more." Lexi says.

"Yeah, in what world?" Adam asks.

"In this one, of course." Lexi says as they both laugh along with me shaking my head at both of them.

"Okay everyone! Time to sing to meee!" I hear a little boy shout. I look over to see it was Johnathan. He was stood on top of the picnic table, a few feet from his birthday cake. I smile as I see Zeke sneak behind him and put his face in Johnathan's neck pretending to bite him. Johnathan laughs and runs to hug Verna's leg. She was talking to a woman I've never seen before. "Daddy's trying to eat me!" He says as he points to Zeke.

"Roar!" Zeke says pretending to be a monster. Johnathan runs from Verna.

"Zeke's a great dad," I hear Lexi say, causing me to turn my attention to her. Her smile fades a bit as she watches them. "It was tough on him after his girlfriend died giving birth to Claire." She informs me. That made me a bit sad. I couldn't imagine...well I guess I can since my mom's been out of the picture for so long.

"Alright everyone! It is time to sing to our birthday boy!" Verna shouts as she catches Johnathan as he tries to run pass her. We sing happy birthday to Johnathan and Johnathan cuts the first slice of cake. I was just finishing the last of my cake when I hear Adam speak.

"You wanna get out of here?" he asks and I nod my head.

Chapter 17

Adam drives me to what looks like the country side of Terry Hills. There was a lot of plain land with nothing but grass and trees. The roads were nothing but gravel and dirt. We arrive at a big white house. On some spots of the house, the paint was peeled and cracked. I look to my right and find a little pond that glistening from the sun. When Adam turns the car off, I give him a look.

"This is our 'get away from home' house. I know it looks like it'll fall apart just by touching it but it's a well and stable house. We stayed here for the whole summer last year. And by "we" I mean my siblings and me. We're going to remodel the house and paint it blue or maybe a pretty dark brown." He says as he gets out of the car. Now, I'm sure any-other girl would have said "Hecks no! There's no way I'm going in there with you." You may be wondering where I stand in the matter, and well I trust Adam. If he says it's safe, then it's safe. He opens the door and I take his hand as he helps me out of the car and into the wheel chair. He pushes me inside the house. The first thing I see is a big living room with a fire place, a wooden table, some couches, and a wooden rocking chair sitting up against the wall. Adam shuts the door and tells me to explore, and that's what I do. This house reminds me of a log cabin. I shiver at that thought. When I was little, my mom's friend Boris, lived in a log cabin in Colorado when he stayed somewhere in the Rocky Mountains. They were always so small and I felt so closed in all the time. When my mom would go visit him I would cry and beg my mom not to take me and of course I'd end up going anyway. I'm currently in a room with lots of old books that are stacked on each-other. They look like they hadn't been touched in ages. I wheel myself to a pile and I notice a book that had "Family Grimoire" written across it. Before I could pick up the book, I hear Adam call my name. I clear my throat loud enough for him to hear and he meets me in the room. He stops at the door and leans on it.

"You're probably wondering what all this is. It's our cousin's. His name is Grant and he is obsessed with witches. They're his favorite fictional fantasy thing." He says with a chuckle at the end. "Sometimes I wonder if he's even related to us." He adds. I'm guessing Grant hasn't been here in a long time, considering the thin layer of dust that covers the top. "You like reading, don't you?" he asks after a few seconds of silence. I nod my head slightly. My attention was still on the book. "Well, if that's the case then I really think you'll really like what I'm going to show you next." He says, causing me to look up at him. He chuckles a bit as walks behind me. I feel him grab onto the handles and before I know it, he's pushing me down the hall. He stops too sudden and tells me to close my eyes. I do as he tells me and he pushes me some more. I hear a door open and he pushes me inside. Once we stop moving, he tells me to open my eyes. When I do, I gasp. The whole room was nothing but a personal library. There were multiple bookshelves everywhere. Don't judge me, I like to read. I go straight to a bookshelf and start my browsing. Adam chuckles. "If you find something you like, it's all yours." He says while walking to a book shelf behind me.

"This one right here, is my favorite," Adam says as I turn around to observe what he was talking about. He holds a black book in his hand, that only had a with a silver heart on the front.

Written on the cover in white words was "Extraordinary". "I read this about a billion times. It's about this town that isolates the middle class, the rich, and the poor. The poor work for the classes above them in this warehouse and they sleep in these underground tunnels. They aren't allowed to go outside the warehouse but this girl; her whole life she's dreamt about knowing what rain feels like. On her 16th birthday and she gets her wish but she also gets caught. So, these "sweepers" which are pretty much police who make sure the poor stay in their area, finds her. She then gets shipped to a different country where she falls in love with a prince and he has to help her find her family." Adam explains. Wow, I think I just might wanna read that. I'm interrupted by my thoughts when I hear glass break and a loud thump coming from above us. Adam whips his head toward the ceiling. "Hide and don't make a sound." Adam orders as he quickly and quietly exits the room. I wheel myself in between a book shelf and a wall. I stay there hoping that no one was up there. Minutes go by and all I hear is the floor creaking above me. "It's okay! It was just a bird!" he yells. A wave of relief washes over me. The last thing we need is a burglar. I come out from behind the book shelf and Adam comes into the room. "I guess I should get some duct tape and seal the whole in the window the bird made. It'll have to do for now plus, it would keep the bugs out." He says. Yeah that does sound like a good idea. I shiver at the thought of sleeping with bugs flying around. They could crawl in your mouth and in your ears. That's my biggest phobia. I can recall a time when I lived in New York, my dad hosted this big house party that was opened to the entire street (not something I'd do). The doors kept opening and closing while letting mosquitoes in. I locked myself in my room and for good measure, I stayed under the covers on my bed. I was so itchy because they were bugs flying around in the house. That night, I couldn't close my eyes without thinking a mosquito was on its' way towards my face for a bite. I'm distracted from memory lane when Adam speaks. "Do you want to keep looking around for books? I could fix us some lemonade before I tackle that window upstairs." He offers and I couldn't agree more. He leaves to go get our drinks and I continue browsing. Out of the corner of my eye, I see something red glowing. It came from in between two books that were close together. I approach the red glow and push the books a part from each-other. There was a red crystal with a black string. It looked like it was made to go around someone's neck. I hesitate, before I picking it up. I find it to be a little peculiar that it was warm like someone had just been holding it. I like this crystal or whatever it was. I gasp at the sudden tingles that shoot throughout my body. I'm too amazed at what I'm seeing and feeling that I almost didn't hear Adam approaching me. I quickly return it back to its' spot. The tingles began to die down but are still lingering. The crystal was no longer glowing and everything looked normal.

"Annabelle?" Adam calls out. I wheel myself out from the book shelf and he hands me the glass of lemonade. I take a sip of it lemonade just as he speaks. "So, did you find anything you like?" I nod my head and point to the five books stacked on top of each-other on the small table by the window. "Awesome. I was wondering if you wanted to um, start soon." He says sounding nervous. I give him a confused look. "I mean with me helping you to get your voice back." He says while rubbing the back of his neck. I tilt my hand side to side to show him I was on the fence about the idea. Truth be told I was nervous. I mean, what if I have a heart attack, a panic attack, and seizure all in one? Okay maybe I'm being a bit dramatic but every time I try to speak, it's like I'm reliving that day my dad shoved peanut butter down my throat. I don't want to go back to that. "Annabelle, we don't have to start at all until you're ready. I just thought wanted to know where you stood on the matter." He reassures me. He must've seen my face. He chuckles a bit and crouches down so that we were leveled. His warm hand touched mine. "If you don't ever want to talk you don't have to. I liked you when you could talk and I still like you now. It doesn't matter to me, just as long as you're happy." He says as he looks into my eyes. He plants a kiss on my forehead. He goes to walk away until I grab his hand. He looks at me and I nod my head. No matter how I look at it, I was going to need my voice at some point in my life. What if there's an emergency and I'm useless? It'll be like that night with Adam all over again.

"Annabelle, you don't have—" Adam start but I cut him off by nodding my head. "Okay. Just let me know when you're ready." He says. Adam tours me around the rest of the house. It was now dark outside and I'm currently picking the books off the table while Adam patches up the window. I look over to where the glowing crystal was to see it wasn't glowing anymore. The tingles were still lingering, but they were more so in my hands and my fractured ankle. I was just outside the library room waiting on Adam. "Alright. That should hold the window for tonight. I'll have one of my brothers help me replace it tomorrow." He says as he walks down the stairs. Before his foot touches the last step, the front door breaks down. I jump at the loudness as I see a black blur fly into Adam. It makes him fly all the way up the stairs. I hear a loud thump along with things being broken. I didn't know what to do and the library door was wide open. It's not like I could go anywhere in a wheel chair. Maybe if I was lucky enough, whatever came in here didn't acknowledge me. I hear a familiar animalistic growl come from upstairs. Fear takes over as I see flashes of Ian and Brody dead on the ground.

The think few seconds, I'm running towards the library. I have to do a double take because I'm actually standing on my own two feet. I hear another growl, followed by a soft thump. Everything was quiet. I was stuck in place with my hand a few inches from the library door. My heart pounds in my chest as I'm once again paralyzed. I then see another blur come in through the front door, but this time it comes towards me. Everything around me is blurred as I move the same speed as the blur. I could only feel wind until I was suddenly pinned against a book shelf. The sudden movement knocks the breath out of me. I flinch when I see the fast-moving blur was a person. This is not happening. This is not happening! Oh my god! What have I gotten myself into? A hand covers my mouth as I look into the eyes in which that hand belonged to. It was a man maybe in his mid-twenties. He had brown eyes and brown hair that was buzz cut He had a nasty scar that was diagonal on his cheek. He wore all black leather that put me in the mind of a biker. He smirks and my heart beats even faster than it was already. He leans in towards me and I close my eyes as I turn my head the opposite direction out of fear. I then feel his hot breath hit my neck.

"What I wouldn't give…" he trails off sounding strained.

"Leave her alone!" a voice I didn't recognize growls out. That voice makes me shiver in fear. It makes me think of one thing, death. I open my eyes as the man turns around to see who had ordered him to leave me be. I feel my stomach drop when I notice it was Adam. His eyes were no longer that smooth light brown I grew used to. Instead, they were completely pitch black. His shoulders rose up and down as he breathed hard. I notice how his shirt is wrinkled and no longer white. His wrists are covered in a black substance. He doesn't look like the Adam I know. He looks like he wanted to kill.

"Adam! Just the person I was looking for." The man says with an Irish accent as he begins to approach Adam. He stops at the door. I look around for a possible way out before my eyes land on the window. I probably won't stand a chance against this guy. In fact, I *know* I won't stand a chance. "I like the new girl. She's so…exquisite. What's her name again? Annabelle, is it?" the man says. My heart drops when I hear my name roll off his tongue. If he knows me, what if there are others out there looking for me? At the thought of that, I'd rather be with my father. I jump when I hear a loud growl. My attention is brought back to Adam and the Irish man. "Aww come on Adam. You know we'd come for her eventually. I mean, after all she does belong with us." The man says.

"Over my dead body." Adam snaps as his eyes turns a pretty blue color. I watch as his nails grow out into claws. His lips are slightly parted and the four tips of his canines are visible. His ears grow until the tips of them are pointy. A little hair extends from his sideburns.

"Well, have it your way." the man says as he goes for Adam. I could not believe what I was witnessing. In a flash, the man was sent flying across the room and makes hard contact with the wooden wall. I'm surprised he didn't just go right through it. He gets up and moves towards Adam in a blur. He pins Adam against the wall with one hand around Adam's throat. Adam growls bearing his teeth at the man. Adam grabs the man's hand that holds him captive and slowly pries his hands off. A horrible crunching sound followed by the man screaming in pain. I look away from them and look at the window. This could be my chance. I could escape! They won't even notice my absence because they're too busy trying to kill each-other. I look over just in time to see Adam slam the man on the table and for it to break. He grabs him again and I can tell he's not done. I wait until they are out of my sight to make my way to the window. When I approach the window to find there weren't any locks on it, I start to panic. How am I supposed to get out now?

"Maybe it isn't locked." I try to convince myself, but I knew it probably was. I push on it and the window doesn't budge. *No!* There has to be another way for me to get out. There has to be. I hear glass break followed by new voices.

"Put him down!" a deep voice yells. It suddenly gets quiet. Hopefully Adam isn't out numbered out there. A red glow in the corner of my eye catches my attention and my body starts to tingle again. I quietly make my way to the glowing light. This leads me to the same necklace that was wedged between the two books on the bookshelf. Giving into the sudden desire to touch the necklace again, I pick it up. I gasp once again as the tingles are more present. What was going on? It made me feel strong. I hear a loud smack followed by a grunt, that comes from outside the room.

"Get out here now! Or your friend here, will have to pay the price." An unfamiliar voice says. I didn't know why, but I didn't want to let go of it. I knew that if I didn't Adam would most likely get hurt or worse. That was enough for me to do as I'm told. I reluctantly return the necklace and slowly make my way out into the room with everyone else. The room is a complete mess. There's shattered glass on the floor, splinters of wood, broken chairs, and a broken table. There's two new guys, plus the Irish man. The two men are twins and they both are brunettes. They looked to be about my age. These brunette twins hold each of Adam's arms as he's on his knees. There's a cut on the side of his forehead that goes all the way to his eyebrow, and a little blood under his nose. The other guy looks to have gotten the short end of the stick. He has blood under his nose and a badly bruised eye. There was a big gash on the left side of his forehead and some dried blood on the corner of his mouth.

"There she is." The Irish man says while smirking. He motions for me with his hand to approach him. I look over at Adam again to see him in his normal state. His brown eyes snap to mine. Concern and shock swirl within his eyes as he sees me walking on my own two feet. "You know, your father's been looking all over for you Annabelle." The man said. The moment he mentions my father, my heart begins racing rapidly in my chest. Flashes of my father shoving peanut butter down my throat fills my mind. I could see the rage behind his eyes when I caught him staring at me. The smell of alcohol fills my nostrils. I shake my head to break free of the haunting visions as I take a few steps back.

"Oh, sweetheart don't worry. We'll take you back to him. I'm sure he'll be thrilled to have you. It'll be like old times." The man says with a smirk.

"If you think I'll let you walk out of here with her, you're wrong." Adam says. The man turns to Adam and punches him in the face. Adam grunts and turns his head towards the man.

Adam's breathing picks up as a deep animalistic growl comes from him. His eyes were now pitch black as he clenches his jaw. The man gets in Adam's face.

"Aw, Did I hurt your feelings?" the teases. Without warning, Adam head butts the man and this causes the man to stumble back. Adam throws the two twins forward by pushing both his arms forward. He was able to get free and he yells at me to run and I listen to his orders. I run as fast as I can. I don't bother looking back. I think this is the fastest I've ever run in my life. I hear grunts and cries of pain come from behind me. I pass by Adam's car and run into the field that's in front of the house. The bad part about being out here was we were in the middle of nowhere and if something bad happened (like what's happening now) there would be no-one to help us. I don't know how long I've been running, but I continue to push myself until I can't anymore. As I stop to catch my breath, I wince as I feel a cramp in my side. Great! Here I am running for my life and I'm worried about a cramp. I lean against a tree as I try to catch my breath. I can't hang out here for long because whatever those men are, they are fast and I'll be dead if they catch me. Fear strikes me as I let the scenes of todays' events unravel and sink into my mind. *He* was looking for me and when he finds me, he he's going to kill me...he's going to kill me... I begin to feel dizzy as I realize that I'm hyperventilating. No, no, no, not this, not here of all places, I'd surely get caught. I close my eyes and take a few deep breaths to calm myself. Both of my hands were on the sides of the tree as if I was hugging it from behind. I let my head touch the tree as I continue to take deep breaths.

"You're okay, it's gonna be okay because I'm gonna get out of here." I mentally tell myself. After a few more breaths, I'm able to calm myself. I open my eyes when I realize how quiet it is. There weren't any frogs croaking or crickets chirping; only the wind rustling through the leaves. That's when I realize Adam wasn't with me...What if they were killing him...what if he's already dead? The thought of his death pains my heart as a wave of guilt washes over me. I think of all the times he's saved me and yet I left him behind. The hairs stick up on the back of my neck as I hear a twig snap on the side of me. I jump and turn in the direction it came from. I stand still trying to listen for any movement. My shaking hand covers my mouth as I try not to panic. Without warning, I'm roughly pinned against the tree. I don't see who my attacker is but it didn't take long for me to guess.

"Now, where were we before we got interrupted?" I hear a very familiar Irish accent say. I'm face to face with the Irish man. If he's here, did that mean Adam was *dead*? The words that come out of his mouth, turns my world upside down. "It's a real shame ya know...He really fought for you...I mean I didn't know he had that much fight in him..." He says smirking at me. There was a lump in my throat and I feel my eyes water. No, no he can't be dead! He can't leave me like this, not after he stole my heart! I feel the warmth of tears rolling down my face. "Oh, don't worry. It was quick." He says with a more menacing smirk than before and I catch a glimpse of what looks like fangs. Wait, fangs? The only word that came to mind was... vampire. *He's a Vampire, and he killed Adam*...Adam's dead and never coming back... I thrash around in attempt to get out of his hold but stop once his hand grips my throat firmly. "I don't want to kill you, but you...you're one of a kind

Annabelle. I don't know if I can control myself..." he trails off, his voice sounding strained as his eyes travel down to my neck. My heart was beating so fast I thought it was going to pop out of my chest. I try to break free by raising my knee to hit him where I was taught to hit in these types of situations. He groans painfully and his grip on me loosens (thanks mom, it worked). I take the opportunity and try to flee but was roughly pinned again against the tree. This time, his grip was tighter and I groan as my back makes contact with the hard tree. "Now, you're making this very difficult for me." He says as he looks at me. The look in his eyes showed that he wanted to hurt me. It instantly reminds me of my father. "Your fathers' orders were to return the package alive and unharmed. But we don't have to tell him about this part..." he says as he roughly jerks my head to the side. I can't move with his iron grip around my throat. As he inches closer, I can't help but think this is my end...

To Be Continued...

Thank you for taking this journey with me into "Annabelle's Beginning" part 1 of the saved series. I hope you have enjoyed the ride with what you have read thus far. If so, be on the lookout for **"Annabelle's Beginning"**, part 2 of the saved series.

Turn the page for a sneak peek...

Saved:

<u>Annabelle's Beginning</u>

Part 2

I raise my knee in attempt to hit him again but he catches my knee with his free hand.

"Not this time sweetheart." He says, his eyes trained on my neck. "I'd hold still if I were you unless you want me to make a mess." He says as he leans in towards me. I don't listen to his suggestion. I squirm around trying to break free but that doesn't stop him. I feel powerless and that makes me want to cry. I feel his hot breath on my skin as his teeth lightly graze my neck. This makes me stop and tremble in fear. I don't want him to bite me and I don't want to be like him (yeah, I've read the books.). "I'm going to enjoy this very much." The man says sounding more strained. Before he has the chance to do anything else, he's yanked off of me. The movement being unexpected makes flinch. Relief, love, and fear fills me as I see it was Adam who pulled him off me. The man flies back into a tree. I hear a loud thud followed by the leaves crumbling beneath him as he lands on the ground. He doesn't move. I'm so happy to see Adam alive and I guess he was too because his lips find mine.

He kisses me passionately and my arms snake around his neck as his hands rest on my hips. He pulls away, and his hands grab both my arms.

"Are you okay?" He asks while observing me.

"I'm fine now that you're here" I think to myself. I nod my head.

"Okay." He says as he winces. Now it was my turn to inspect him. I notice his shirt was torn a bit by his side. It's soaked in blood. I look up at him. "I'm fine. It's nothing that can't be fixed." He breaths out from the pain. I almost cry at how happy I was to see him alive. I don't even want to think about him not being here. Before I can stop myself, I press my lips to his. I pull away and close my eyes as I hug him, taking in the faint smell of his cologne. That moment is short lived when the cool breeze reminds me where we are...alone in the dark with the Irish vampire. Adam turns around to the man who's faced down on the ground. I grab his arm and he looks at me. "I have to make sure we aren't followed. I don't want to do this but if it means keeping you safe and alive, then that's what—" Adam's cut off when he's tackled by the man...

About the Author

I was born on February 14th in Detroit Michigan, where I lived for 13 years. In 2011 I moved to Texas where I work part-time while attending college. I have always had an undeniable passion for writing. There are so many stories and characters in my head and I can't wait to share them with you. This passion began in the fifth grade. My mom would always buy my siblings and I journals as a way to express our feelings. From there I began to write poems which later turned into short stories, and now my first novel. I'm very proud of this accomplishment, for I know this is just the beginning.

CPSIA information can be obtained
at www.ICGtesting.com
Printed in the USA
FFOW03n0355130518
46541576-48554FF